F

TC

KUR    AN

CW00767387

# THE FREEDOM TO THINK KURDISTAN

James Kelman

thi **wurd**
thi-wurd.com

First published in Glasgow, Scotland in 2019 by thi wurd

This edition first published in this format 2019 by thi wurd

Copyright © James Kelman 2019

The moral right of James Kelman to be identified
as the author of this work has been asserted by
him in accordance with the Copyright, Designs
and Patents Act 1988

Book only ISBN  978-0-9931758-5-5

eBook ISBN  978-0-9931758-6-2


British Library Cataloguing-in-Publication Data
A catalogue record for this book is available from the British Library

Cover design by Andrew Cattanach

Designed and typeset by Biblichor Ltd, Edinburgh

Printed and bound by Clays Ltd, Elcograf S.p.A.

*You must insist on living.*
*There may not be happiness*
*but it is your binding duty*
*to resist the enemy,*
*and live one extra day.*
                    *(Nâzım Hıkmet)*

*For the great Estella Schmid*
*who worried the hell out of me,*
*and aye got the work done*

# Contents

# Introduction

The essays gathered here relate to the struggle of the people of Kurdistan, written over a number of years. They derive mainly from talks I prepared and delivered at public meetings: where content is lifted from one to another, a few repetitions are unavoidable.

In recent years attacks on the Kurdish community have been carried out in this country by Police Scotland. It is inexcusable, and shameful. They serve to highlight not simply the ignorance of the police (to give them the benefit of the doubt) but the ignorance of the wider public. I include here people who earn a living within the media and political establishments. They cannot be excused on the grounds of ignorance.

During September 2017 one such attack occurred in Edinburgh, capital of Scotland and seat of the Holyrood Government. A couple of weeks later I was in a library and there was a conversation going on between three staff members, quite a loud conversation. I tried to focus on the book I was browsing. Then the name 'Turkey' cropped up and I eavesdropped.

They were not discussing fascism, censorship and suppression; police and state brutality, the destruction of historic sites, of cities and towns; the links between gangsterism, the far-right and Government individuals; the imprisonment of foreign journalists and their own elected political represent-atives, disinformation and propaganda, the hundreds of thousands of people dead or left bereft . . . None of that, they were discussing sandcastles, sunny beaches, and the cost of return flights to the sun-kissed shores. They were extolling the virtues of Turkey as a holiday destination.

I considered saying something but what was there to say? I would have tried not to be sarcastic, not to be angry, neither to condescend, nor to patronize. I hope I might have tried to inform them, in some way. But where to begin? I could not face it and instead exited the building.

Such is the complexity of the Kurdish struggle for justice, for survival, I would not have known where to start. Perhaps I could have jumped in with something about the current situa-tion in Rojava, and referred to 'democratic confederalism', noting briefly the constant stream of disinformation from the Turkish State and their allies on Abdullah Öcalan and the Kurdish Workers' Party (PKK). I could have touched on Syria; perhaps on Iraq and the move to independence in Iraqi-Kurdistan. That would make reference to the situation in Iranian Kurdistan. A brief note there on Mahabad and the short-lived independent republic of Kurdistan back in 1946 – which is not all that old, surely, since it was the year I was born, when the last of the nomadic Kurdish tribesmen were still trying to move freely on the old routes, coming from the Black Sea area through the Caucasus mountains, following a route that touches on the borders of these separate nation-states, routes they travelled for a couple of thousand years before finally, halfway through last century, most of the remaining Kurds were forced to submit, voluntarily or by compulsion, by force of arms. It is estimated that 10,000 Kurdish tribesfolk alone were killed by Iranian forces, in the aftermath of the Second World War . . .

My awareness of the plight endured by Kurdish people began in May 1991 when I was invited to contribute to a public meeting organized by the Friends of Kurdistan in Edinburgh. The subject was language, culture and oppression. The talk began from my own country which is Scotland, widening the context to finish on the dire reality confronted by the Kurds. In those days I needed to write a paper for such an event. Once it was written that was that and no turning back. But I knew I had misjudged the audience. The event took place in the university, in the David Hume Building, and I prepared my talk for an audience of students and academics. In the event 90% of those present were Kurdish.

As the night wore on it became apparent that political divisions existed within this community but no room was allocated for a debate arising from that, which at the time I found odd. Maybe this was for the sake of a united front. Or the platform-speakers – myself included – went on far too long. Iraqi-Kurds had hosted the evening. At the end there was a general sense of dissatisfaction. So much to discuss, so little time to do it. Whatever it was I found the evening difficult. No wonder. The subject is massive and my knowledge was then so very slight.

I used the experience to explore some basic problems in offering solidarity for later meetings organized by the Friends of Palestine in Glasgow, by European Action for Racial Equality and Social Justice held in Southall, Middlesex and for a fringe meeting on racism organized by black members of the National and Local Government Officers' Association. Thus the first essay in this collection, 'Oppression and Solidarity', is an amalgam of talks I was asked to give in contexts that might be described as alien to a white middle-aged Glaswegian protestant-bred atheist father of two.

The idea that differences might have been aired in the space of a two-hour meeting at Edinburgh University only indicates my naivety. But that was 30 years ago. My interest developed especially in east and southeast Turkey, where

> the Kurdish settlement area comprises the 23 vilayets (departments) of eastern and southeastern Anatolia and the Kurdish districts of Sivas and Marash covering an area of about 230,000 square kilometres. The territory, which the Kurds call Northern Kurdistan (Kurdistana Bakur), had 12.2 million Kurds in 2016 . . . [T]here are also strong Kurdish communities in the big Turkish metropolises like Istanbul, Izmir, Ankara, Adana and Mersin . . . Assuming an average estimate of eight million Kurds in the Turkish part of Turkey, thus arrives at the figure of 20 million Kurds in Turkey, about 25% of the total population of this country . . . Some Turkish demographers predict that if the current high Kurdish birth rate should continue, the Kurds could by 2050 constitute the majority of the population of Turkey. Hence the policies of forced displacement towards the west of the country in order to assimilate (Turkanize) the largest possible number of Kurds in order to avert this "peril".[1]

In my earliest reading I was impressed by Abdullah Öcalan and the PKK. Many were of my own generation, coming to adulthood during the 1960s and 1970s. Their interest in external struggles and liberation movements in general would have been influenced by the politics and intellectualism of the day. Nowadays this would be termed 'extreme left', then it was merely 'radical', or 'alternative', humanitarian. People across the globe saw it was possible to challenge hegemony, whether in Vietnam or in Chile. In those far-off days the PKK were one more liberation group. Their criminalisation occurred a few years later.

I continued the basic reading I had begun for that first Edinburgh meeting back in 1991. I learned of the worldwide Kurdish diaspora, counting in hundreds of thousands, perhaps as many as two million. There were Iraqi-Kurds, Iranian-Kurds, Syrian-Kurds and Turkish-Kurds. Neither was it inconceivable that I might meet with a Russian-Kurd, given that people who identified as Kurds were in Armenia and in Azerbaijan.

Some older maps referred to a geographical body by the name of 'Kurdistan'. Here was a country that did not exist, with a definite outline: a 'complete' Kurdistan. I found that exciting. Why did it never appear in newer maps? Was it a matter of political expediency? I used the image of the neck and head of a horse to remember the shape. I could draw a line enclosing southeast Turkey, northern Syria, northern Iraq, northwest Iran and note how the northeastern section of Turkey 'linked' into southern Georgia and Armenia. This line is an outline, is unbroken and may be described as a border. It was straightforward to visualize such a territory as a country. If people called it a country I would not have disagreed. But why would people call it a country if it was not a country? Why would they have to?

The more I learned the more obvious it was that if Kurdistan was not a country then it should have been and would have been, all things being equal. But all things are not equal and here lies more than a hundred years' history.

The Kurdish struggle is part of radical history as any struggle for liberation is but how can this particular history remain such a secret? Must it remain a secret? The Kurds refuse to be buried. Those of us who are not Kurds should not look away. If we wish to delve further there is much to learn, much to discover.

I recommend immediately an essay by Mehmed Uzun[2]. This will advise you that there is not just a country but a nation whose name is Kurdistan. Didn't you know this? Why didn't you know this? What are the defining qualities and attributes of a nation? How do we recognize a nation? For those who know nothing at all begin from Uzun's essay.

Away and find it yourself.

There are some very great Kurdish artists but I don't know who they are. Uzun's essay will not offer a list of those. His essay will offer himself. From this we make an inference: where there is 1 there is 2, perhaps 4, or 16, or 256, or 65,596.

How many artists are there in Kurdistan? How many people? How many children? What languages do they speak? What do their people do and how do they live, and where do they come from? And is it mountains and flatlands they have? Are there rivers and lochs? What are their songs and their stories?

In the last interview given by Abdullah Öcalan before his incarceration, more than twenty years ago, he was asked to account for 'the PKK's bad image'. At the time fifteen Kurds were on trial in France 'accused of being terrorists'. Öcalan was quite matter-of-fact in his reply: "France is making a lot of concessions to Turkey. Politics are often based on material interests. We, the Kurds, we have nothing to give . . ."

I disagree. For several decades the people of Kurdistan have been giving themselves. Not long after the interview Öcalan was betrayed and captured, and has remained in prison ever since. This prison is located on İmralı island. There is nothing else on this island except this prison. There is only one prisoner in this prison on this island. He is Abdullah Öcalan. There was no word of him for years. Was he alive or dead? We did not know. We asked the question. They declined to answer. Did anyone know? Yes. The Turkish State and the 'powers' close to them. Who are the 'powers' close to them? It turns my stomach to name them. Go and find out for yourself. Start at Holyrood then visit Whitehall[3]. For eight long years his lawyers were blocked from seeing him.

The Turkish State does what it chooses to do. They are asked to stop. They choose not to. Petitions are delivered to their president and their leaders. They decline to answer. This is how it is and how it has been since the end of the First World War. For the past hundred years the Turkish State has sought to eliminate all things Kurdish from the territory: "Wave after wave, without interruption . . . separating families, relatives, tribes . . . destroying villages, settlements. In the snow of winter, in the heat of summer. Without a pause."[4] Horrible tragedies: rape, torture and assorted barbarism; extra-judicial killings, massacres, genocide; the grossest iniquities: in parallel, the collusion and political corruption, the hypocrisy and cynical self-interest of the 'powers' closest to Turkey: Great Britain, France and the USA.

In 1997 Amnesty International invited me to attend The Freedom for Freedom of Expression Rally in Istanbul, and report on it for them. Also present from the United Kingdom was the novelist Moris Farhi, a member of the PEN International Writers in Prison Committee, working on behalf of imprisoned writers throughout the world. Moris was born in Turkey and it must have been particularly difficult for him in the circumstances. We were among twenty foreign writers making the trip to Istanbul; six were from Israel.

Turkey is run by the military and one surely is entitled to describe the country as fascist although the majority of the population in the UK seem ignorant of the reality; a similar level of ignorance will apply in France, in Russia and in the USA, given that the vast majority of US arms transfers to Turkey have been subsidized by US taxpayers.[5] Of the $10.5 billion in US weaponry delivered to Turkey since the outbreak of the war with the PKK in 1984, 77% of the value of those shipments – $8 billion in all – has been directly or indirectly financed by grants and subsidized loans provided by the US Government. In the same 1999 document we read that "Turkey's F-16 assembly plant in Ankara – a joint venture of Lockheed Martin and Turkish Aerospace Industries (TAI) – employ[ed] 2,000 production workers, almost entirely paid for with US tax dollars." In another report from 2018 we were advised that

Russia will deliver its S-400 missile defense system to Turkey despite the US State Department's decision to sell a rival platform to Ankara for $3.5 billion.

The S-400, a mobile long-range surface-to-air missile system, is the Kremlin's answer to America's Patriot and

THAAD platforms. Lockheed Martin makes the THAAD or Terminal High Altitude Area Defense System, while Raytheon makes the Patriot.

Last year, Ankara signed an agreement with Moscow for the S-400 missile system, a deal reportedly worth $2.5 billion. All the while, Turkey has helped finance America's most expensive weapons system, the F-35 Joint Strike Fighter.[6]

The Turkish State is backed not only by Russia and USA, collusion with its National Security Council is rife throughout Europe, including the United Kingdom. One effect of this is the difficulty in obtaining information. The southeast of Turkey is the northwest of Kurdistan but word from the interior is suppressed inside the country. In the United Kingdom it is impossible to obtain adequate news if you rely only on the mainstream media. The level of ignorance among the population, although staggering, is unsurprising, consistent with British State policy.

I recall the day after a young Turkish Kurd was murdered in a racist attack on the streets of Glasgow in 2001 that the Turkish football team Fenerbahçe arrived at Glasgow Airport to play their UEFA cup match at Ibrox Park.[7] The BBC local news bulletin reported the arrival and headed the programme with a demonstration by more than a thousand predominantly Kurdish refugees in the centre of Glasgow. They then cut to the Turkish football team and the Turkish travelling support at Glasgow Airport, two separate pieces of news, and the impression was given that Turkey is just an ordinary European country, that there is no possible link between it and the hundreds of thousands of Kurdish refugees across the world, not to mention the dead youth, murdered only three weeks after arriving in Scotland.

European football supporters travel to Turkish cities and tens of thousands continue their sunshine package-holidays to safe resorts on the Turkish coast. Meanwhile the curtain is draped solidly across the southeast of that same country to suppress all news of the horrors being perpetrated upon women, children and men, where

> neither the right of law, nor human rights, nor democracy is adhered to. Instead what we see are fear and poverty, and suffering. Everywhere are swarms of armoured cars, tanks, and other military vehicles, identified and unidentified; tens of thousands of soldiers and security personnel, uniformed and plainclothed. This is a war-zone.[8]

When I visited Istanbul in 1997 in the foreign writers' delegation, our primary purpose was to present ourselves to the State Prosecutor with a 'declaration of crime' in solidarity with the people then being prosecuted by the Turkish State Security Court for doing precisely the same thing several months earlier. The UK media showed no interest whatsoever in this unique show of solidarity. None at all. Nothing was reported. Yet inside Turkey itself the presence of twenty foreign writers at that inaugural Freedom for Freedom of Expression Rally was a major media happening.

Demonstrations and protests in Turkey are banned by the National Security Council (the military). The way folk get round it is to call a press conference and then throw it open to all; and everybody attends, including the security forces in full battle gear. At that 1997 event the organizers called one such 'press conference' and three to four thousand people turned up, including approximately two thousand heavily armed troops.

Not all twenty writers presented themselves to the State Prosecutor but the majority did so. It was to highlight the case of the great Kurdish writer Yaşar Kemal who "in January 1995 was tried in Istanbul's No. 5 State Security Court regarding one of his articles which was published in *Der Spiegel* magazine."[9] For this 'thought crime' Kemal was convicted of 'inciting hatred' and received a twenty-month suspended sentence. I became acquainted with the work of Yaşar Kemal as a young fellow browsing the Ks on the library shelf – Kafka, Kemal, Kerouac – wondering where I would go when my first book came out, and quite happy sharing the K shelf. I didn't expect to go to jail which is where so many writers wind up in the Republic of Turkey.

By the mid 1990s the writer and sociologist İsmail Beşikçi had spent around 17 years of his life in prison for exercising 'the freedom to think'. The Turkish National Security Council does not concede such 'freedoms' to its general population. In 1998 I was invited to a conference held in Hamburg by the Kurdish Parliament in Exile. For my contribution I delivered a paper entitled *Em Hene!*[10] The essay included here is a later, revised version of that.

The exploration of the identity of the Kurdish people has been the lifetime work of Beşikçi, advocating their right to self-determination. In return he received sentences of between 70 and 200 years imprisonment by the Turkish

11

military authorities. Another couple of years seemed to get tacked on every other week. His 33 publications are banned as 'thought crimes'. In 1999, benefit nights took place in Glasgow and Edinburgh to raise awareness not only of Beşikçi's plight but of the factors governing his imprisonment. His publisher Ünsal Öztürk had just been released from prison and managed to come from Turkey for these events. He spoke at both events; also present on both evenings was Neville Lawrence, whose family's campaign sought justice for the loss of his 18-year-old son Stephen, murdered in London by racists.[11]

In 2000-01 we held other solidarity events and Şanar Yurdatapan travelled from Turkey to lend his support[12]. It is absolutely crucial to mention here that neither Beşikçi, nor Öztürk, nor Yurdatapan is a Kurd, all three are Turks.

Around this time I gave students of Creative Writing at the University of Glasgow an essay by Mehmed Uzun. This was the one he delivered to the State Security Court No. 5, Istanbul. I was trying to give an idea of the situation facing writers (and publishers) in other countries, and the extreme danger they confront on a daily basis simply for doing their best, whereas if they keep their mouth shut they do well, and progress in their 'careers'.

When I was teaching in the USA some students became angry when I gave them work by foreign writers that appeared to suggest all was not well with the world. They were even more dumbfounded when I gave them work by their own writers who suggested the same thing. They were of the generation taught to ridicule Noam Chomsky. But some listened and some delved further.

Twenty-odd years ago the Turkish State regarded Beşikçi as its second most dangerous man. The man occupying prime position was, and remains, Abdullah Öcalan, President of the PKK. Öcalan is held in İmralı Island prison off the Turkish mainland under sentence of death. How he landed there is a complicated story.[13] But according to an 'unnamed' representative of Turkey's most powerful supporter, the USA, "We spent a good deal of time working with Italy and Germany and Turkey to find a creative way to bring him to justice."[14]

Öcalan offered his own account of his capture: "that the NATO central headquarters had played the essential role," and not Turkey. When he landed in Kenya – wherein he was captured and taken to Turkey – it was through the machinations of the Greek Government. The Greek Ambassador met Öcalan in Nairobi and confided to him: "I was leading the NATO unit which had been after you for twenty years; while searching for you in the sky I found you in my hands."[15]

At a more recent press conference, relayed by his lawyers to a press conference on İmralı Island, Öcalan spoke of the need to form "democratic alliances between political parties in Turkey not simply [towards] an election [but as] developed between various parties while Europe was in transition to democracy . . . A lesson must be learned from the solution of Scotland, Ireland, and Wales . . ."[16]

In the Republic of Turkey, and all 'powers' in collusion with them (the UK, Saudia Arabia, Russia, Israel, Germany, France, Italy, the USA and so on) the advocacy of something as mild and puny as 'the Scottish solution', means a person is an 'evil terrorist'.

Even to conduct a dialogue towards the creation of a

devolved parliament would require a change in the law. Even to refer to the situation of Scotland or Wales in relation to Kurdistan in Turkey is a crime. "Not one sentence can be uttered in defence of the Kurds, or of the Kurdish leader, without the charge of 'separatism' or 'terrorism' being levelled."[17] It exemplifies the farcical nature of the so-called Trial at which Öcalan, honorary chairman of the Kurdish National Congress, was tried as a criminal, found guilty and sentenced to death.

They have yet to carry out the sentence.

I thought it a marvellous gesture when the University of Strathclyde Students' Association in Glasgow granted Honorary Life-Membership to Öcalan.

People are repulsed by the actions and behaviour of the Turkish State, and repulsed also by the cowardice, the collusion and the utter greed of those 'powers' who might act to change the situation. And still the Turkish State does what it wants to do and will not stop until forced to do so. For several decades people have detailed atrocities, massacres, rapes and tortures, even genocide. Analyses are performed, statistics presented and algorithms formulated.

Well done.

Meanwhile the tyrants continue to do what tyrants always do, whatever they like. Petitions are presented, and so on. It happened yesterday, and the day before, and the day before that too, and will continue tomorrow and the next day and the next day, and on and on and back and forth and meanwhile the Turkish State will do whatever it chooses to do.

For those of us who wish to demonstrate solidarity and have no personal connection to Kurdistan and the Kurdish people the danger is being overwhelmed by reality. There is so much data, so little time. How do we make sense of it? The truth is we cannot hope to make sense of it. We should not label such a 'hope' as 'forlorn'. The 'hope' is not forlorn. We cannot make sense of the horror. We do our best to end it.

I am wary of the concept, 'taking lessons from history' but I make exception for one: do not negotiate with the tyrant.

Many years ago Abdullah Öcalan and others within the PKK were interested in Scotland, as they were in any struggle grounded in issues around the validity and survival of indigenous languages and culture; issues around self-determination, 'home rule' or independence. Nowadays Turkish-Kurds have moved to a position that some would argue better reflects their circumstances. They have shown a pragmatism that some find staggering, and very exciting. The friends of Kurdistan, and there are hundreds of thousands of us throughout the world, have followed the extraordinary situation in Rojava and wondered how is it possible. These Kurdish people and their various communities, their friends and their comrades are offering a way ahead that is not only coherent, consistent and utterly pragmatic, it is humane, it is revolutionary. No wonder State authority cannot cope.

Whatever we do we cannot continue to gather information, as though to lay out evidence for a supreme and benign authority. There is none, not in this world. So it serves no purpose. Worse than that, it drains our energy. We have to move with what we have.

Vedat Türkali, another Kurdish writer, said in reference to his work as a novelist that he was "hard to please, but I know that being fond of perfection is a dead-end street." He was making the point about a novel he had written, that the finished result might not have been as good as he hoped, but he had to jump in and write it, then stop, and move on. Revision is eternal, if we allow it. As in art, so too in learning, we make stuff. We learn and we make. The resources available through the internet reach the point of saturation. We need to stop prior to that. Otherwise we do nothing. Gathering information becomes an end in itself. We can all be students. But we must stop the study to write the essay. Learning leads to making, and this includes making sense. We use what we have and push ahead. And while pushing ahead we make even more sense. This is radical history. We have to do it ourselves. It is my hope that the essays in this pamphlet will help provide an introduction to the historical background.

# Oppression and Solidarity

Certain ethnic groups are well treated by the dominant nations only to the extent that these groups accept abandoning their culture, their mother tongue, their history and their literature, in other words to the extent that they accept assimilation. We have a duty to encourage these ethnic groups to oppose assimilation, to develop and enrich their mother tongue, their literature and their culture. Only in this way can world culture develop, enrich itself and serve humanity.

*Article 18 of the Statutes of the Human Rights Commission*

This is fine as far as it goes, but I always wonder who the 'we' are. The one thing I do know is that this 'we' never refers to the oppressed and suppressed groups under discussion. They are not so much the subject of Article 18 as the object. They do not get a say in the matter. Things get done to them. The 'we' of Article 18 have a choice: they can treat oppressed groups well or not well; they can encourage or not encourage. But no matter what that 'we' decide it is their decision. The rest of the world have to put up with it.

*Article 18 of the Statutes of the Human Rights Commission* is as good a definition of western liberalism as you will find. From pronouncements such as this you can tell why

European civilization has produced so much theology and philosophizing on action and non-action, ethical debates on individual and collective obligation, social and otherwise; reasons for and against personal responsibility; an entire edifice of educational and social structures designed to deal with whether 'we' have a duty to do this, that or the next thing. Not designed to perform these 'duties', just to deal with the question of whether 'we' have them or not, as an adjunct to 'our' continuing exploitation and ruthless acts of destruction.

It could only happen within a hegemony, where one community has assumed power and has absolute control over other communities. Communities under attack never have these particular ethical worries, they just find ways of defending themselves.

It should go without saying that any culture, history or literature is valid. Or any mother-tongue. Let's call it language; even using the term 'mother-tongue' in this imperial context somehow renders it invalid, an inferior 'salt-of-the-earth' type thing. It should be an obvious point that we can't use terms like superior or inferior when we speak about cultures and languages, not unless we're willing to use these terms about actual people. If we feel happy describing persons or peoples as inferior then by all means we can use these terms when we speak of their cultures or languages.

Of course in our part of the world these so-called obvious points aren't recognized as obvious at all. Not only are they not recognized as obvious, our society is premised on the opposite view; our society is premised on the 'fact' that one culture is superior to another, that one language is superior to another, one literature superior to another, one class superior to another: that one people is superior to another. That's the fundamental premise which sets the structural basis of our society, it's endemic to it, it informs everything within it, from law and order to education, from health to housing to immigration control. And because of that when for example a racist violation takes place on the streets it is entirely consistent that it should do. If the state is racist why should we act as though racism on the street is some sort of aberration? We live in a racist state so it's consistent. Why should we act as if it's a kind of social phenomenon?

But when we talk about the hegemony of English culture we aren't referring to the culture you find down the Old Kent Road in London, we aren't talking about the literary or oral traditions of Yorkshire or Somerset: we are speaking about the dominant culture within England; the culture that dominates all other English-language based cultures, the one that comes from within the tiny elite community that has total control of the social, economic and political power-bases of Great Britain. And leaving aside the USA's sphere of influence this is also the dominant culture throughout the majority of English-speaking countries of the world.

There is simply no question that by the criteria of the ruling elite of Great Britain so-called Scottish culture, for example, is inferior, as the Scottish people are also inferior. The logic of this argument cannot work in any other way. And the people who hold the highest positions in Scotland do so on that assumption. Who cares what their background is, whether they were born and bred in Scotland or not, that's irrelevant, they still assume its inferiority. If they are native

Scottish then they will have assimilated the criteria of English ruling authority; if they hadn't they wouldn't have got their jobs. Exceptions do exist but exceptions only make the rule.

So of course Scotland is oppressed. But we have to be clear about what we **don't** mean when we talk in these terms: we don't mean some kind of 'pure, native-born Scottish person' or some mystical 'national culture'. Neither of these entities has ever existed in the past and cannot conceivably exist in the future. Even when arguments involving these concepts are 'rational', they can only be conducted on some higher plane. And it's always safer for human beings – as opposed to concepts or machines – when this higher plane is restricted to mathematics, theoretical physics or logic (or else religions that insist on a fixed number of gods). The logic of this 'higher plane' generates a never-ending stream of conceptual purity to do with sets and the sets of sets; and the sets of the sets of the sets of sets; and the set of the sets of the sets of all sets. In the earlier days of humanity we might substitute 'set' for 'god', and seek the god of all gods.

Entities like 'Scot', 'German', 'Indian' or 'American'; 'Scottish culture', 'Jamaican culture', 'African culture' or 'Asian culture' are material absurdities. They aren't particular things in the world. There are no material bodies that correspond to them. We only use these terms in the way we use other terms such as 'tree', 'bird', 'vehicle' or 'red'. They define abstract concepts; 'things' that don't exist other than for loose classification. We use these terms for the general purpose of making sense of the world, and for communicating sensibly with other individuals. Especially those individuals within our own groups and cultures. When we meet with people from different groups and cultures we try to tighten up on these loose, unparticularized definitions and descriptions.

If you happen to be a Scotsman in a Scottish pub and you get talking to another Scottish man and you ask where he comes from you don't expect him to say 'Scotland', you expect him to say 'Glasgow' or 'Edinburgh' or 'Inverness'. And if you're a Glasgow woman in a Glasgow pub and you meet another Glasgow woman and you ask where she's from you expect her to say 'Partick', or 'the Calton', or 'Easterhouse' or whatever. And if you're a Dennistoun man in a Dennistoun pub and you meet another Dennistoun man and you ask where he comes from you don't expect him to say 'Dennistoun', you expect him to name a street or say 'round the corner' or 'Alexandra Parade' or 'Onslow Drive' etc.

Once in my company a white working-class guy got into an argument with a black middle-class guy, a writer who had been doing a reading then during the follow-on discussion spoke of the historical culpability of white people in relation to black people. It was quite brave because this was in Glasgow and the audience was 95% white. The white working-class guy lost his temper and called him a black bastard. He was out of order to do so and there isn't any excuse. But the black guy was also out of order. Both were wrong. There is a simplistic, generalized version of history which offers a sweeping account of the inhuman savagery perpetrated on black people by white people. There is a tighter version wherein the inhuman savagery is perpetrated by white peoples. An even tighter version concerns the inhuman savagery perpetrated on black peoples by white peoples. And so on. There is also the daily abuse and violation experienced by black people that is beyond anything white people can comprehend. There is also the day-to-day horror of existence experienced by a great many white Glaswegian people that a great many black people, including this particular black guy (who is an academic as well as a writer) have no conception of. His blanket use of black and white, in context, served only to indicate his intellectual myopia about the everyday brutalities the British State perpetrates on sections of its own people, its so-called white brothers and sisters. White nationalism or black nationalism, it always misses the point.

Wherever you look either at home or abroad you find cultures under attack, communities battling for the right to survive – often literally, where the fight for self-determination means not only putting your own life on the line, it's risking and endangering the lives of your people and your family and your friends and your children. This is a war that's being waged and engaged on countless fronts. And these heavy defeats will continue until authentic and meaningful honest dialogue starts occurring between the countless communities and peoples under attack.

In an interview with İsmail Beşikçi – held while he was awaiting trial in a Turkish prison in 1990 – he referred to the prosecution of the Kurdistan Workers' Party (PKK) which took place in Germany the same year, and reported on the "secret agreement between the NATO alliance and Turkey in relation to Kurdistan". Covert deals are always being done of course. This one means the Ankara Government is entitled to do anything it likes under the heading 'Rooting Out The PKK'. For the actual people in Turkish Kurdistan it means they would rather flee across the Iraqi border than remain at home, they would rather confront Saddam Hussain's forces than stay and face the Turkish authorities.

> About 15 years ago a group of Kurdish students [once] published a tract demanding that incitement to racial hatred be made a punishable offence and were charged with having claimed that there was a Kurdish people, thereby undermining national unity.[1]

The students had published the tract in response to various anti-Kurd threats made publicly from right-wing sources, including one nationalist journal implicitly threatening the Kurdish people with genocide. Meanwhile, and since the end of the First World War, the authorities have sought to destroy everything which might suggest a specific Kurdish identity, not just in Turkey but in Iraq, Iran and Syria. Different theories about nationhood have been constructed, essentially 'to prove' the non-existence of the Kurdish people, that they are not and never have existed.

The plight of the Palestinian people derives from similar historical factors, following the break-up of the Ottoman Empire and the end of the 1914-18 war. Like the Kurds, they have witnessed the theft of their land and resources, their very identity; the mass slaughter of countless human beings. The people of Asia, Australasia and Africa have their own stories the horrors of imperialism and the continuing effects of this.

The black and immigrant communities in the UK need no reminder of the primary role of the British State. Here too other home communities are under attack. In Glasgow the incidence of asbestos-related terminal disease is nearly eight times higher than the UK average. 15 members of the Clydeside Action on Asbestos group have died since the turn of the year [at the time of writing, around early spring of 1992]. I'm talking about ordinary working people in so-called ordinary working conditions, conditions that ultimately killed them.

There is constant pressure on this support group. They receive no help from the official Labour movement, not the Scottish Trades Union Congress (STUC) and not the Labour Party; not from any left wing party or group. They exist on donations from victims and sympathizers. Their major battles are against lawyers and the legal system, doctors and the medical profession; insurance companies and the asbestos industry, and one primary arm of state control, the Department of Social Security (DSS). The British authorities always deny that the asbestos these victims were exposed to is at the root of their various, essentially fatal diseases, contracted through no one's fault but that of their employers who knew the danger but didn't tell them, in direct contravention of government legislation, knowingly and cynically.

Even in Glasgow where around 20,000 people have contracted asbestos-related terminal diseases since the end of 1945 very few people are aware of the reality of the nightmare faced by their neighbours and relatives, a nightmare that will become worse, and is not reckoned to hit a peak for at least another generation. The State distorts and disinforms. Side-by-side with the asbestos industry and the big insurers the authorities stop the information process, dishing out their propaganda. So most victims die of a disease the State says they haven't got. And as long as they deny the disease that's killing these thousands of people throughout the country the DSS avoids having to pay out the disablement allowances and entitlements due to the victims. They avoid the people of the country knowing the full horror of a tragedy that could have been averted, given that those who perpetrated the tragedy – the asbestos multinationals – have been in full cognisance of the deadly nature of asbestos fibre, at least since the 1890s, while continuing to stuff our schools, factories and hospitals full of it.

Activists within black and immigrant communities here in Britain will soon pick up on the **general form** of the asbestos struggle. It's only in the last 10 years, in the wake of the New Cross Massacre (as John La Rose and others point out) that the State has conceded racism might be a motive in violent assault and murder. Even so they fight tooth and nail to deny it on each and every occasion. Just as **each and every** victim of asbestos-related industrial disease must fight to demonstrate the cause of his or her imminent death, so too must a victim of racist violation fight to demonstrate that the people responsible for the violation were motivated by race-hatred.

No life or death struggle takes precedence over another.

Speaking with folk from different parts of the colonized and otherwise oppressed world, and with folk from within the different black communities and the different groupings here in Britain, one crucial problem lies in being honest with one another.

At some point people from overseas have to appreciate why many left wing, sympathetic people in this country just look nonplussed, embarrassed or depressed when asked to send off letters and petitions to Labour Party MPs and councillors and trade union officials. It's not that making representation to our elected and constitutionally attested representatives might not be a good move, as far as *your* particular struggle is concerned; but within *my* struggle, here in Glasgow, within the context of its culture(s), such a move is absolutely worthless, a waste of time and resources – akin to a contradiction in terms. That's my opinion though it rarely gets expressed, for at least two reasons, the first of which is dubious; I don't like being presumptuous. The second reason is that *you* have said such a move is crucial. And I'm aware or should be aware, that a decision made by those involved in one struggle is determined ultimately by its own context, that one solitary compromise, even with ruthlessly brutal states like that of the British, South African, Turkish, Israeli or USA, may save hundreds, even thousands of lives. When a compromise like that needs to be made it cannot be made outwith the context of that struggle and that struggle alone. This doesn't mean only those born and bred within the culture of that struggle have the right to make such decisions. But generally it does mean that. So when an outside group or community seeks support in an approach to our domestic ruling authority, generally, we have an obligation to go along with the request, no matter our reservations.

It is fundamental that the general struggle for human rights is shown solidarity by those engaged in other struggles. A too rigid adherence to one line or idea or theory is a hindrance. More often than not this rigidity just indicates an unwillingness to accept that particular struggle in itself; an unwillingness to accept what should be the inalienable rights of those engaged within that struggle, the right to fight as they see fit, in a context that ultimately is theirs and theirs alone.

There's nothing more ridiculous than these so-called radical left-wing parties coming along to some demonstration or protest apparently in solidarity, then spending their time arguing with the people out doing it on the street, about the theoretical incorrectness of their ideological approach, their lack of awareness of 'the international context'. I'm reminded of that one about the guy selling – I can't remember – Newsline or Militant or the Morning Star or Living Marxism or Socialist Worker or the Workers' Hammer or whatever the hell, at the time of the printworkers' battle with Rupert Murdoch (and the British State) a couple of years ago. A small group of workers had overturned a car in preparation to defend themselves against the forces of law and order, the comrade boys-in-blue, and this guy goes up and tries to tell them the Tories are the class enemy while at the same time forcing his newspaper down their throats.

But that doesn't mean we give up discussion and go in for blanket gestures of solidarity. Every struggle has a context. Every struggle has its own culture. The mistake we make is not discussing our differences, at the right time and the right place. For our part we have to take the bit between our teeth and make sure refugees and exiles don't mistake the official labour movement as the left in Britain, while at the same time allowing them to make representation in that direction. It's pointless being huffy. That also applies to those who ask for support. You have to understand why many of us don't turn up or don't get invited to demonstrations of solidarity organized by the official Labour movement. We all assume too much. We don't like being presumptuous. But we have to risk all that. It doesn't mean making decisions for other people and criticising them when they make a move that doesn't square with our own perspective – if we continue on that path then all talk of solidarity remains just that – talk; the sort of humbug you hear from party hacks everywhere.

I remind people here this evening, especially the ones who've got a copy of a recent *Glasgow Keelie* in their pocket, that the police confiscated as much of this issue as they could get their hands on.[2] Suppression of this nature is part of the reality of contemporary Glasgow. The first thing to acknowledge is what's happening under your nose.

(1991)

# The Freedom for Freedom of Expression Rally/ Istanbul 1997

The arrogance of [the Iranian King] Jamshid had set his subjects in revolt against him, and a great army marched towards Arabia from the highlands of Iran. They had heard that in Arabia there was a man with a serpent's face that inspired terror and to him they went in order to elect him as their king. Zuhak eagerly returned with them and was crowned . . . Jamshid fled before him, and for a hundred years was seen by no man, till Zuhak fell upon him without warning in the confines of China and put him to death. Thus perished [Jamshid's] pride from the earth.

For a thousand years Zuhak occupied the throne and the world submitted to him, so that goodness died away and was replaced by evil. Every night during that long period two youths were slain [whose brains provided food for the serpents that grew from Zuhak's shoulders] . . . It happened that [there remained two men of purity, of Persian race who] succeeded in entering the king's kitchen. There, after no long time, they were entrusted with the preparation of the king's meal, and they contrived to mix the brains of a sheep with those of one of the youths who was brought for slaughter. The other one they saved alive and dismissed secretly, saying to him: "Escape in secret, beware of visiting any inhabited town; your portion in the world must be the desert and the mountain."

In this manner they saved two hundred men, of whom is born the race of Kurds, who know not any fixed abode, whose houses are tents; and who have in their hearts no fear of God.

Abul Kasim Mansur Firdawsil (935 – 1025 AD)

This three-day event, the Freedom for Freedom of Expression Rally, was organized and hosted by the Freedom of Thought initiative, a 200-strong group of artists and activists. There is a multiple trial in progress in Istanbul: writers, musicians, actors, journalists, lawyers, trade unionists and others are being prosecuted by the State Security Court. Twenty international writers attended the rally; most are members of PEN but three travelled at the invitation of Amnesty International, including myself.

More writers are imprisoned in Turkey than in any other country in the world[1] but "the real question [is] not that of freedom for a writer. The real question is that of the national rights of the Kurds."[2] The annexation of Kurdistan, the attempted genocide and the continued oppression of the Kurdish people are three of the major scandals of this century. Historically, the British State, if not prime mover, has had a pivotal role.[3] At one point 'we' needed a client-state "to secure ['our'] right to exploit the oilfields of Southern Kurdistan," and so 'we' created a country, gave it a king, and called it Iraq.[4] 'Our' active participation in the assault on the Kurdish people continues to the present where 'we' retain a leading interest in diverse ways, e.g. client-state of the USA, member of NATO, member of the European Union, etc. Turkey itself "is now the number two holiday destination for UK holidaymakers thanks to superb weather, great value for money accommodation, inexpensive eating out and lots to see and do."[5]

Prisoners are routinely tortured and beaten in Turkey, sometimes killed. Rape and other sexual violations occur constantly. In the Kurdish provinces the mass murders, forced dispersals and other horrors practised by the security forces are documented by many domestic and international human rights agencies. People have been made to eat excrement. From Kurdish villages there are reports of groups of men having their testicles tied and linked together, the women then forced to lead them round the streets. There are files held on children as young as twelve being subject to the vilest treatment. This from a 16-year-old girl detained not in a Kurdish village but by the police in Istanbul:

> They put my head in a bucket until I almost drowned. They did it again and again . . . They tied my hands to a beam and hoisted me up. I was blindfolded. When I was hanging I thought my arms were breaking. They sexually harassed me and they beat my groin and belly with fists while I was hanging. When they pulled down on my legs I lost consciousness. I don't know for how long the hanging lasted . . . They threatened that they would rape and kill me. They said I would become paralysed. The torture lasted for eight days.[6]

The young girl was later charged with being a member of "an illegal organisation". Germany, the USA and the UK compete to supply war and torture implements to the Turkish security forces who learned about the efficacy of the hanging process from their Israeli counterparts. A student we were to meet later at Istanbul University was once detained for twenty-four hours and during that period she too was tortured.

There exist "152 laws and about 700 paragraphs . . . devoted to regulating freedom of opinion." The Turkish Penal Code "was passed in 1926 . . . [and is] based on an adaptation of the Italian Penal Code . . . Its most drastic reform was the adoption in 1936 of the anti-communist articles on 'state security' from the code of Mussolini. Only in April 1991 were some changes made through the passage of the Law to Combat Terrorism." Before then, and up until 1989

court cases against the print media had reached a record level with 183 criminal cases against 400 journalists . . . at least 23 journalists and editors in jail with one of them receiving a sentence of 1,086 years, later reduced to 700 on appeal. The editor of one [well-known journal, banned by the Özal dicta-torship] was prosecuted 13 times and had 56 cases brought against her. She was in hiding at the time the journal[7] appeared in July of 1990. One of her sentences amounted to six years, three months. Despite international appeals and protests the Turkish Government refused to reverse her sentences. No left-wing or radical journal was safe from arbitrary arrest, closure or seizure of entire editions. Police persecution extended into the national press and included daily newspapers. Authors and publishers of books were victimized. In November 1989 449 books and 25 pamphlets were burned in Istanbul on the orders of the provincial governor . . . [Until] 1991 189 films were banned . . . [and during the following two years came] the liquidation of journalists, newspaper sellers, and the personnel of newspaper distributors, as well as bombing and arson attacks against newspaper kiosks and bookstores . . . [In 1992] twelve journalists were murdered by 'unknown assailants' [and] in most cases, the circumstances point to participation or support by the state security forces. [In 1994 writers and journalists were sentenced to] 448 years, 6 months and 25 days . . . There were 1162 violations of the press laws [and] a total of 2098 persons were tried, 336 of whom were already in prison . . . The security forces interfered with the distribution of press organs, attacked their offices, and arbitrarily detained publishers, editors, correspondents and newspaper salesmen.[8]

Shortly before the Military coup in the spring of 1991, I took part in a public meeting organized by the Friends of Kurdistan.[9] I looked at parallels in the linguistic and cultural suppression of Kurdish and Scottish people, and that was a mistake.[10] Parallels between the two may be of some slight functional value from a Scottish viewpoint but when we discuss the Kurdish situation now and historically we are discussing the systematic attempt to wipe from the face of the earth a nation of some 30 million people. It is doubtful if any form of oppression exists that has not been carried out on the Kurdish people and I think the scale of it overwhelmed me. I combined some of the elements of my 1991 talk with those of others of the same period, and published an essay.[11] I now give an extract from my notes for that talk, as a brief introduction to how things were for Kurdish people before the 12 September military coup back in 1980:[12]

The Turkish Republic set up its apparatus for the repression of the Kurdish people soon after it was founded. Following the War of Independence, during which they were acclaimed as 'equal partner' and 'sister nation', the Kurdish people found their very existence was being denied. The authorities have since sought to destroy everything which might suggest a specific Kurdish identity, erecting an entire edifice of linguistic and historical pseudo-theories which supposedly 'proved' the Turkishness of the Kurds, and served as justification for the destruction of that identity.

These theories have become official doctrine, taught, inculcated and propagated by the schools, the universities, the barracks, and the media. The authorities banned all unofficial publications that tried to even discuss the subject. Historical or literary works, even travellers' tales published in Turkish and other languages, were all removed from public and private libraries and for the most part destroyed if they contained any reference to the Kurdish people, their history or their country. All attempts to question official ideology were repressed.

It is estimated that 20 million Kurds dwell in Turkey and the Kurdish language has been banned there since 1925. In 1978, of all Kurdish people over the age of six, 72% could neither read nor write. The publication of books and magazines in the language is illegal. The Turkish authorities purged the libraries of any books dealing with Kurdish history, destroyed monuments and so on.[13] All historical research into

Kurdish society was forbidden. An official history was constructed to show the Kurdish people were originally Turks. Until 1970 no alternative research could be published. Thus officially the Kurds are purest Turk.

The Turkish authorities have systematically changed the names of all Kurdish towns and villages, substituting Turkish for Kurdish names. The word 'Kurdistan', so designated from the 13th century, was the first to be banned; it is regarded as subversive because it implies the unity of the scattered Kurdish people. Kurdistan is colonized not by one country but by four: Turkey, Iran, Iraq and Syria whose Chief of Police published a study [in November 1963 which] set out to 'prove scientifically' that the Kurds 'do not constitute a nation', that they are 'a people without history or civilization or language or even definite ethnic origin of their own', that they lived 'from the civilization and history of other nations and had taken no part in these civilizations or in the history of these nations.' [He also] proposed a 12-point plan:

1) the transfer and dispersion of the Kurdish people;
2) depriving the Kurds of any education whatsoever, even in Arabic;
3) a 'famine' policy, depriving those affected of any employment possibilities;
4) an extradition policy, turning the survivors of the uprisings in Northern Kurdistan over to the Turkish Government;
5) a divide and rule policy; setting Kurd against Kurd;
6) a cordon policy along the lines of an earlier plan to expel the entire Kurdish population from the Turkish border;

7) a colonisation policy, the implantation of pure and nationalist Arabs in the Kurdish regions to see to the dispersal of the Kurds;

8) military divisions to ensure the dispersion;

9) 'collective forms' set up for the Arab settlers who would also be armed and trained;

10) a ban on 'anybody ignorant of the Arabic language exercising the right to vote or stand for office;

11) sending Kurds south and Arabs north;

12) 'launching a vast anti-Kurdish campaign amongst the Arabs'.[14]

Media organs are the property of the official language in Turkey, and the Kurdish people are kept starved of outside news. Kurdish intellectuals are expected to assimilate, to reject their own culture and language, to become Turkicized. A person from Kurdistan cannot be appointed to fill a post without the prior approval of the political police. Kurds are not nominated for jobs in the Kurdish provinces; the authorities try always to separate them from their own country.

All business is conducted in the language of state and Kurdish speakers must use interpreters. Literature produced in exile, beyond the Turkish borders, is not allowed into the Republic. Kurdish writers and poets have had to write in Turkish, not simply to ensure publication but because they were unfamiliar with their own forbidden language and culture.

For a brief period a group called the Organisation of Revolutionary Kurdish Youth (DDKO) was tolerated by the authorities; this group set out to inform public opinion about the economic, social and cultural situation; organising press conferences and public briefings, publishing posters, leaflets etc., focussing attention on the repression within Kurdish areas; its monthly ten-page information bulletin had a print run of 30,000 which was distributed amongst Turkish political, cultural and trade union circles, as well as in Kurdish towns and villages. Eventually 'news' about what was happening to the Kurds filtered through to the media and the public and there were protests against the repression. Six months before the military coup of March 1970 the leaders of the organisation were arrested and after that all 'left-wing parties and organisations were outlawed.'

But from 1975 new youth organisations formed, known generally as the People's Cultural Associations (HKD), concentrating on educating their members and helping peasants and workers who were in conflict with the authorities in one way or another. A policy of terror and ideological conditioning was implemented by the Ankara Government which in the words of Turkish sociologist İsmail Beşikçi managed to 'make people believe he who announced 'I am Kurdish' was committing a crime so heinous that he deserved the death penalty.' Dr Beşikçi was put on trial for the crime of 'undermining national feelings' and 'making separatist propaganda.'

In the same talk I drew attention to the interview İsmail Beşikçi had given while in prison awaiting yet another trial. He had remarked of the German prosecution of the Kurdish Workers' Party (PKK), that the one thing established was the existence of a "secret agreement between the NATO alliance and Turkey, in relation to Kurdistan." Germany has now fallen into line with the Turkish State and has declared the PKK an illegal organisation: even to sport their colours is a criminal offence. The victimisation of Kurdish people has spread outwards, we are witnessing the attempted criminalisation of the entire diaspora.[15]

Throughout Europe there are incidents being reported by monitoring agencies. In November in Belgium "100 police and members of the special intervention squad . . . raided a Kurdish holiday centre . . . The Ministry of Justice claimed [it was] used by the PKK as a semi-military training camp." Nobody at all was arrested. But forty people were deported to Germany. On 2 February of this year (1997) "the Danish television station, TV2, revealed that the Danish police intelligence service (PET) had written a 140 page report on meetings of the Kurdish parliament in exile which took place in Copenhagen in March 1996 [and the] transcript . . . ended up with the Turkish authorities."[16]

Here in the UK, Kani Yılmaz is halfway into his third year in Belmarsh Prison, London. He came from Germany in October 1994 at the direct invitation of John Austin-Walker MP, to meet with British MPs and discuss cease-fire proposals between the PKK and the Turkish armed forces[17]. In a shameful act of betrayal the British State responded by arresting him. Germany wants him extradited and Turkey waits in the wings. Sooner or later they will find a way to sort out 'the extradition problem', thus the British can hand him back to Germany who can hand him back to Turkey. Or else they might just cut out the middle man, this would be their ideal situation.

Olof Palme of Sweden was assassinated more than 10 years ago; it so happens he was also the only European leader who ever confronted the Turkish State at the most fundamental level, by "recognising the Kurdish people as a nation and [committing] himself to attaining recognition of their rights."[18] It would be comforting to suppose that the British and other European Governments and state agencies act as they do through sheer cowardice. Unfortunately I doubt if this is the case. The Turkish State has the means of authoritarian control for which many Euro-state authorities would cut off their left arm. In certain areas they draw ever closer, for example in matters relating to asylum and immigration; their punishment of the most vulnerable of people; the torture that takes place in prisons and police-cells, the beatings, the killings. And not too long ago

on 14 February 1997, the [British] government attempted to introduce a private members' bill, the Jurisdiction (Conspiracy and Incitement) Bill, which would have had the effect of criminalising support for political violence abroad. It was only defeated when two left Labour MPs, Dennis Skinner and George Galloway, unexpectedly forced a vote on the third reading and caught the government unawares, as they were relying on cross-party support for the Bill.[19]

In October 1996 came the report on Lord Lloyd of Berwick's Inquiry into Legislation Against Terrorism, published "with very little publicity and only a brief press-release, an inquiry into counter-terrorist legislation . . . set up jointly by Home Secretary Michael Howard and Secretary of

State for Northern Ireland Sir Patrick Mayhew. Such is the terrorist threat," says the report "that not only is permanent legislation desirable to combat terrorism, but past powers need to be further widened and strengthened." The expert commissioned by Lord Lloyd "to provide 'an academic view as to the nature of the terrorist threat' [was] Professor Paul Wilkinson of St Andrews University." His 'academic view' provides Volume 11 of the report whose

> new definition of 'terrorism' is modelled on the working defi-
> nition used by the FBI: 'The use of serious violence against
> persons or property, or the threat to use such violence, to
> intimidate or coerce a government, the public or any section of
> the public, in order to promote political, social or ideological
> objectives.'[20]

No later than one month after its publication, "amid allegations of financial losses" the *Mail on Sunday* named the
professor as a "terrorist expert in college cash riddle". Then
came the more interesting information, that Professor
Wilkinson was "believed to work for the British security
services and the CIA." There is one thing established by the
fact that Wilkinson is still commissioned for work as sensitive as the Lloyd report, this is the contempt held by the
British State not just towards the public but its elected
representatives.

His connections were something of an open secret before
this; readers of *Lobster* magazine have known of his pedigree
for at least ten years, in particular his "inept role in the state's
attempt to discredit Colin Wallace in the 1980s."[21] This was

when "disinformation was run into the Channel 4 News office" by Wilkinson, two members of the UDA plus "a former colleague of Wallace" at the Information Policy Unit in HQ Northern Ireland.[22]

Notwithstanding any of this the 'terrorist expert's' credibility is undiminished and as I write, following the day of transport stasis in London,[23] one of Scotland's two 'quality' daily newspapers, *The Glasgow Herald*, again features the Professor's 'academic view'; on this occasion he proposed that "to defeat their terrorist tactics, British and Irish security must target the godfathers of the IRA's crimes" and not give in to such tactics as "bringing a complex transport system to a halt . . . Any group of clever dicks in an open society could achieve that . . ."

The juridical system in Turkey may be complex but its central purpose seems straightforward enough, it sanctifies the state and protects it from the people. Following the 1980 coup and throughout the next decade changes in the law took place, the mechanisms for the suppression of Kurdish people altered. For the Kurds it became one nightmare after another. The level of state-sponsored terrorism degenerated to a point where sometime between 1981 and 1983, in Diyarbakır Prison, forty Kurdish youths were tortured to death for refusing to say "I am a Turk and therefore happy."[24]

We have to respect the fact that it was not until 1984 that the PKK began its armed struggle. If we do not then we play into the hands of the Turkish propaganda machine. The new constitution had come into existence in November of 1982 and an indication of the potential repression is available there, e.g. this from the opening preamble:

no thought or impulse [may be cherished] against Turkish national interests, against the existence of Turkey, against the principle of the indivisibility of the state and its territory, against the historical and moral values of Turkishness, against nationalism as defined by [Mustafa Kemal] Atatürk, against his principles, reforms and civilizing efforts . . .

Not only is the possibility of democracy denied at the outset, it is illegal even to think about something that might be defined by the constitution as 'against Turkish national interests'. The system is so designed that any Turkish Government, courtesy of the constitution, is in thrall to a higher authority: the National Security Council (i.e. the military).

Some might argue that 'Turkish democracy' is designed solely to suppress the Kurdish population and it would be presumptuous of me to argue the point, especially with Kurdish people. But if justice is ever to be achieved by the Kurds in Turkey perhaps it will come about through the will of the majority of the people, and the majority is Turkish. Münir Ceylan, one of the contributors to the Freedom of Expression publication makes the point that "if you analyse the Anti-Terror Law carefully, it is obvious that [it] is intended to destroy the struggle for bread, freedom and democracy not just of the Kurdish people but by our entire working class and working masses."

It seems that among Turks there has been an increase in solidarity with the Kurdish people, and also a willingness on the part of many to confront one of the world's most ruthless state-machines. The courage and perseverance of Beşikçi surely have been crucial in this. Next to Abdullah Öcalan, President of PKK, the National Security Council appears to regard the sociologist and writer as its most dangerous enemy. Beşikçi is not Kurdish, but Turkish. Since 1967 he has been in and out of court and has suffered "arrest, torture, jail, ceaseless harassment and ostracism."[25] Now 57 years of age he has spent nearly fifteen years of his life in prison. Each time an essay, book or booklet of his is printed he is given a further term and so far the aggregate stands at more than 100 years. Under Turkish law his publisher is prosecuted simultaneously and to date has received sentences in the region of 14 years. Less than two years ago the two men "were abused [and] physically assaulted while being conducted from prison to the court . . . [and their] documents . . . rendered useless."[26]

There is a distinction between the people of a country and its ruling authority. The Turkish State is not representative of the Turkish people and neither is the British State representative of myself or Moris Farhi from England who was there in Istanbul on behalf of PEN International Writers in Prison Committee. My invitation to the Freedom for Freedom of Expression Rally came from Amnesty International (UK), by way of Scottish PEN. Although not a member of either body I was glad to accept. There were 21 foreign writers present and each of us would have been conscious of the relationship to Turkey held by our individual countries: the Netherlands, Germany, the UK and Sweden supplied two apiece; one each from the USA, Mexico, Canada-Quebec, Finland and Russia; one writer represented Palestinian PEN, whereas six writers came from Israel. The multiple trial of writers, artists and others which is now in process derives from January 1995[27] when

Yaşar Kemal was tried in Istanbul's No. 5 State Security Court regarding one of his articles which was published in *Der Spiegel* magazine. On the same day, intellectuals gathered outside the court in support [and] decided to collude in the 'crime' by jointly appending their names to [that and other] articles and speeches alleged to be 'criminal'. The "Initiative Against Crimes of Thought" was born [and] a petition started. Within a short time the signatures of 1080 intellectuals from various fields had been collected [and they] co-published a volume of articles entitled *Freedom of Expression*. Under the Turkish Penal Code Article 162: republishing an article which is defined as a crime is a new crime, and the publisher is to be equally sentenced ... On 10 March 1995 the 'co-publishers' voluntarily presented themselves before the State Security Court to face charges of 'seditious criminal activity'.[28]

Thus the state authorities were challenged at a fundamental level, leaving the Turkish Government "with the old dilemma: either democratize the law and the constitution or face the opposition of Turkish and world democratic opinion, and the stench of another major scandal."[29]

There is scarce room for bureaucratic manoeuvring in the Turkish system and if a 'crime' has been committed there is little option but to prosecute. If not then the prosecutor himself is open to prosecution.[30] So far the *Freedom of Thought* initiative has forced the hand of the authorities to the extent that the State Security Court has had to bring to trial one hundred and eighty four people. It is known as the 'Kafka Trial' and has been described as "the most grotesque farce in Turkish legal history." Even so, the state makes use of its power and "for the accused [it is] likely to result in 20 months' prison sentences." Some of them are already in receipt of suspended sentences for earlier 'criminal' thoughts or statements and their periods of imprisonment will be even longer.

The next step taken by the campaign organizers was to produce an abbreviated form of the *Freedom of Expression* publication, and then invite international authors to sign up as 'co-publishers'. In principle the repressive nature of the Turkish legal system does not allow foreigners to escape the net, even on foreign soil. By using a network based on PEN International Writers in Prison Committee and other human rights agencies the campaign's organizers managed to obtain the signatures of 141 writers as 'co-publishers' of the booklet. But this time the State Security Court declined to prosecute "on the grounds that [they] would not be able to bring [the international writers] to Istanbul for trial . . . because such an 'offence' does not exist in US or English law." (Perhaps not yet. I take nothing for granted.)

So the campaign organizers moved a stage further: they invited some of the international writers to come to Istanbul in person, and present themselves at the State Security Court. Again using the network of PEN and other human rights agencies they asked that invitations be issued on their behalf. The twenty one of us present included poets, film-makers, novelists and journalists. Interest in the 'Kafka Trial' had escalated within Turkey; at each public engagement there was a full-scale media presence.

On Monday morning more than half of us were in court to witness the trial of an actor, one of the 1080 Turkish writers, artists and others who signed as 'publishing editors' of the original *Freedom of Expression*, the collection of writings by authors either already in prison or due to stand trial. Yaşar Kemal has received a 20-month suspended sentence for his own contribution to the book. But the actor's trial was postponed until May, presumably when no international observers will be present. Meantime he continues rehearsing a joint production of Genet's *The Maids* and Kafka's *In the Penal Colony* and hopes to be at liberty to take part in the performances.

Following the postponement some of us were due at Bursa Prison; the authorities were allowing us to visit Beşikçi and his publisher, Ünsal Öztürk. Others were scheduled to meet Ocak Işık Yurtçu, a journalist imprisoned at Adapazarı. Then permission was reversed by the authorities, we could make the journey if we wanted but we would not be allowed to speak to the prisoners. It was decided we would send a 'symbolic' delegation. A majority of us volunteered to make the journey but places were limited to three, and two went to Bursa Prison. Louise Gareau-Des Bois was nominated to visit Adapazarı. She is vice president of Canada-Quebec PEN and also speaks a little Turkish; seven years ago the Quebec centre seconded a Kurdish PEN resolution concerning Beşikçi. When she arrived at the prison the authorities reversed their previous reversal and she was allowed to talk with Yurtçu through a fenced area for nearly twenty minutes. What disturbed her most was the great number of young people behind bars, some little more than boys.

We were in court for a second occasion with Moris Farhi who was signing his name to the abbreviated version, *Little Freedom of Expression*. The State Prosecutor dismissed his declaration out-of-hand. The third time we arrived at the State Security Court a dozen of us were there on our own behalf. But a heavy contingent of police had been instructed not to let us enter the gate. The prosecuting authorities were refusing to accept our statements, not even if we sent them by registered post. We held a press conference outside on the main street and signed our statements in front of the television cameras. Münir Ceylan was there with us. He is a former president of the petroleum workers' union and from 1994 served twenty months imprisonment for making statements such as the one quoted above. Recently he received a further two year sentence and expects to be returned to prison any day now. His case has been taken up by Amnesty International, supported by the Scottish Trades Union Congress. He and others walked with us to the post office, in front of the television cameras, where we sent our signed statements by registered mail.

If the authorities continue to refuse our names alongside those of the Turkish writers and other artists who have been on trial then the initiative's organizers will attempt to have the State Prosecutor charged with having failed "to fulfil the constitutional commitment to equality of treatment." It is a bold campaign and puts individuals at personal risk; some have been threatened already, some have experienced prison, others expect it sooner or later. On the same afternoon we had a public engagement at Istanbul University. A forum on freedom of expression had been organized by students and a few sympathetic lecturers. About twenty young people came to meet us then escort us to the campus; four of their friends are serving prison sentences of eight to 12 years for 'terrorist' activities.[31]

Every day at Istanbul University between 100-200 police are on campus-duty and the students have their bags searched each time they enter the gate. Along with us on the bus came Vedat Türkali,[32] a famous old writer who spent seven years in prison for political activities. He remains a socialist and is now domiciled in England. When we arrived we discovered not only had the forum been cancelled by the security forces, they had shut down the actual university. More than two thousand students had gathered in protest outside the university gates. We were instructed to link arms and march as a body, flanked by students on either side, straight to the gates of the university.

Hundreds of police in full riot-gear were also present. The cancelled forum on freedom of expression had become the focus of a mass student demonstration, the underlying concerns being the current withdrawal of subsidized education and the continued victimisation of the student population. I could not see any tanks although occasionally they are brought in on student-protests. When we got to the gates at the entrance to the university the riot-police circled and sealed us off. Some student representatives, lecturers and the media were allowed into the circle with us. A few held banners, an act of 'terrorism' in itself, and were requested to fold them away, not to provoke the situation.

After negotiations with the security forces it was agreed that an abbreviated press conference could take place with the international writers and that statements might be broadcast to the students via a loud-hailer. Demonstrations are illegal in Turkey unless permission has been granted by the security forces. Most people have given up seeking permission; instead they organize a press conference and invite everybody. A female student opened the meeting then Şanar Yurdatapan[33] spoke, calling for everyone to stay calm, no blood should be spilled under any circumstances. Next to speak was the lawyer of the four imprisoned students, Pelin Erdal, one of whose own relatives was raped during a period of detainment. Only about a dozen of the 21 international writers were present at this 'press conference' and each one was introduced. The situation was extremely tense and time restricted. Joanne Leedom-Ackerman (vice-president of PEN International) and Alexander Tkachenko (president of Russian PEN Centre) were delegated to speak, and they were given a great ovation by the students. Then we had to leave at once, linking arms to stay as closely together as possible, returning quickly the way we had come.

There was no news of any bloodshed although we did hear that a disturbance and arrests had taken place in the area of the post office, after we had left the scene earlier in the day. That evening we attended a reception held for us by the Istanbul Bar Association. A few lawyers are among those openly expressing their opinions on the issue of freedom of thought and expression. We met Eşber Yağmurdereli, lawyer, writer and playwright, at present "appealing against a 10-month sentence [for referring] to the Kurdish minority." He is also under suspended sentence from an earlier case; if he loses the appeal he will face "imprisonment until 2018."[34]

It was at the same reception we heard that Ünsal Öztürk, Beşikçi's publisher, had just been released from prison. He came to our last official engagement, described as "a meeting of writers and artists, organized by Turkish PEN Centre, The

Writers' Syndicate of Turkey and the Association of Literarists." However, there was little opportunity of a meeting as such. Twelve or more people spoke from the platform during the two hours, including some of the international writers. For some reason Öztürk was not invited to speak. Nor for that matter was Türkali. I mentioned to a member of Turkish PEN that it might have been worthwhile hearing what Türkali had to say and was advised that in Turkey there are 'thousands like him', whatever that might mean.

I thought it also of interest that Şanar Yurdatapan was not invited to speak. Yurdatapan and his brother, his secretary and a translator, were our four main hosts and escorts throughout the four- to five-day visit, ensuring we remained together in the various awkward situations. He is one of the central organizers of this campaign and has served previous terms of imprisonment. He also led an international delegation to probe the notorious Güçlükonak massacre of "11 men travelling in a minibus." According to official sources they were killed by the PKK, but the "investigations left little doubt that government security forces carried out the killings."[35]

We also met Ünsal Öztürk and his wife socially on the last night. They sat at our table for a while, giving information through an interpreter to Soledad Santiago of Mexico's San Miguel PEN Centre who was hoping to take up his case through the PEN International Writers in Prison Committee, although he is a publisher and not a writer. Like Münir Ceylan and others, Öztürk is liable to be re-arrested at any moment and I found it difficult to avoid watching his wife who seemed to be doing her best not to watch Ünsal too often and too obviously.

The next morning it was time to fly home to 'freedom and democracy'. For the flight into Turkey I had been advised to take nothing that might be construed as political – especially 'separatist' – propaganda. For the flight to Glasgow via Amsterdam on Thursday afternoon I was also careful. During the past days students had given me diverse literature to take from the country but the situation by this time had become extremely sensitive. In the lounge of our hotel that morning only four of the 21 remained, passing the time before being driven to the airport. People there were showing more than particular interest in us, and doing it in shifts. I thought it better not to take chances, and so I dumped the diverse literature.

When we left I bought three English-language newspapers. One carried a report on the introduction of torture in USA prisons; the other had a front-page-lead on the arrival of a new prison ship off the south coast of England – which may prove opportune for Turkey's justice minister who recently complained of "a negative atmosphere about Turkey. But now we will monitor human rights in Europe. The only thing Europe does is criticize Turkey. However, from now on we will criticize Europe."[36]

In Article 18 of the Statutes of the Human Rights Commission the language itself is exclusive, where 'we' have "a duty to encourage ethnic groups" whose culture is under attack but the 'ethnic groups' under attack are somehow left out of the equation. Perhaps 'we' do have a duty, but it is to stand aside and let 'them' fight back in whatever way 'they' deem necessary. Perhaps the real duty 'we' have is not to interfere when 'they' resist oppression.

I also accept the significance of the distinction between 'democratic rights' and 'human rights': 'democratic rights' – unlike civil liberties or human rights – "assert the rights of the people to struggle against exploitation or oppression;" the right to defend yourself under attack, it allows of empowerment, of self determination. I accept the right to resist oppression and that this right is inviolable. The people of Turkey and/or Kurdistan will resist oppression in whatever way they see fit. I can criticize the form this resistance sometimes takes but I am not about to defend a position that can only benefit their oppressors.

Almost nothing of contemporary Turkish writing is available in translation via English-language UK or USA publishing channels. As far as I know, not even Beşikçi's work has managed to find a publisher.[37] At Glasgow's version of a press conference, organized by Amnesty International (Scotland) and Scottish PEN on the morning after my return from this extraordinary event in Istanbul only one journalist turned up. This was an embarrassed young guy from *List Magazine*, a fortnightly entertainment listings magazine. A couple of weeks before my visit to Istanbul *The Scotsman* newspaper had included the following snippet in a rare UK report on Turkish domestic affairs:

> Turkey's armed forces have intervened three times in the past 37 years to restore law and order in the country and to safeguard its secular nature.

# A Press Conference in Turkey

*At the gates to the university, surrounded by riot troops.*
*Şanar Yurdatapan is on megaphone.*

Some writers from PEN International were here in solidarity for the Freedom for Freedom of Expression event. The writers are surrounded by riot troops. James Kelman stands two back from Şanar Yurdatapan and behind him is one of the riot troops. This was a 'press conference'; the only method the citizens had available in Turkey to hold a public meeting. The other writers here include Alexander Tkachenko (front row second left) and Joanne Leedom-Ackerman (front row far right).

Among Turks at this period there was an increase in solidarity with the Kurdish people, and also a willingness on the part of many to confront one of the world's most ruthless state-machines. The courage and perseverance of Beşikçi was crucial in this. Next to Abdullah Öcalan, president of PKK, the Turkish National Security Council appeared to regard Dr Beşikçi a sociologist, as its most dangerous enemy. Beşikçi is not Kurdish, but Turkish. Since 1967 he had been in and out of court and suffered "arrest, torture, jail, ceaseless harassment and ostracism."

*Here writers from the PEN delegation are awaiting a*
*visit to Bursa Prison to meet with İsmail Beşikçi.*

Beşikçi's 33 books were banned and he had received sentences totalling more than 100 years in prison (by 1997) for "thought-crimes", his advocacy of the national rights of the Kurdish people. The visit to meet him was cancelled by the authorities. Other writers with Kelman in this photograph include Louise Gareau-Des Bois (vice president, Quebec PEN Centre, Canada); Joanne Leedom-Ackerman (vice president, International PEN); and Soledad Santiago (San Miguel PEN Centre, Mexico).

*The poor quality of this image is due to the fact that the pamphlet was produced in photostat form to replicate the original but with the addition of the named foreign writers as 'co-editors'. Under existing Turkish Law, all writers whose names appeared as co-editors were in breach of the Law.*

# Em Hene!

Some people find it possible to support campaigns on behalf of writers imprisoned for their political beliefs without worrying about the substance of these beliefs, why the writers are imprisoned in the first place. They know next to nothing about the writer's culture, community or society and manage not to regard such knowledge as fundamental to the campaign. It follows that they agitate for the cessation of human rights abuses without inquiring why the rights of these particular human beings are being abused in the first place. At the time of writing in Turkey there are many writers in prison but if one writer is being victimized for daring to give expression to a 'dangerous thought' it is likely that tens of hundreds are in the same plight, perhaps tens of thousands, with none but their family and friends to fight and campaign on their behalf. The writer and sociologist İsmail Beşikçi has spent nearly 15 years of his life in prison. He argues that those who campaign on his behalf must recognize that the campaign cannot be about one writer, it is about the existence of Kurdistan, it is about justice for Kurdish people.

Abdullah Öcalan is President of the Kurdish Workers' Party (PKK) and until his capture in Italy was one of the most wanted men in the world.[1] For the majority of the Kurdish people he is a hero. Beşikçi has maintained that Öcalan is a legitimate leader of the Kurdish people. In the first report I read of Öcalan's capture the pro-Turkey bias was blatant, straight from the public relations department of the National Security Council. It is still a surprise when distortion and propaganda of this magnitude come unchallenged in the mainstream media. This example arrived via Associated Press (AP) thus would have appeared not only in the US but in the UK and elsewhere in the 'free' world. One comment sticks with me, that there have been "no executions in Turkey since 1984". That kind of rubbish is just disgraceful. Who knows the number of executions committed in Turkey since 1984? State executions are also 'extrajudicial', defined as the "unlawful and deliberate killings of persons by reason of their real or imputed political beliefs, ethnic origin, sex, colour or language, carried out by order of a government or with its complicity [and] take place outside any legal or judicial process."[2]

Human rights organisations will have approximations of the number. There can only be approximations. It is estimated that between 1991 and early 1997 there were "more than 10,000 'disappearances' and political killings."[3] Each Saturday in Istanbul women and girls gather in the famous old thoroughfare of Galatasaray to bear witness to the 'disappearance' of husbands, boyfriends, fathers, sons and brothers. The courage of these women and girls is quite something, there are hundreds of them. Most are Kurdish but a few are Turkish. Sometimes the police just wade in and batter them with riot-sticks, whether observers are there or not.

Football fans will recognize Galatasaray as the name of a leading Turkish football club. The stadium is not too far away and this area is at the heart of Istanbul's tourist quarter. Holidaymakers and football fans are surprised that the women are battered right out in the open. Some look the other way. This is encouraged by the British political authorities who, when they are not supporting the Turkish State in a less passive manner, take care not to look themselves. It is only a few months since the end of that other sorry saga, the British Government's cowardly, but ruthless, treatment of Kani Yılmaz.

As mentioned in an earlier essay the man was arrested on his way to address a meeting in London. It was not until the summer of 1997 that he was finally extradited to Germany to face charges of organising attacks on Turkish businesses and properties. The Labour Government's Home Secretary was Mr Jack Straw who

> ignored campaigners' pleas and upheld the court order for his extradition. Yılmaz had spent almost three years in detention in Belmarsh prison. The decision, following the House of Lords' rejection of his petition against the extradition, was a slap in the face to supporters who believed that Straw would carry his opposition convictions into government; Straw was one of several Labour MPs who protested strongly when Yılmaz was arrested and detained for deportation on 'national security' grounds on his way to a meeting at Westminster in October 1994.
>
> That arrest had caused embarrassment to the Tory Government because Yılmaz had been allowed into the country freely days beforehand: the German Government's action in seeking his extradition was widely seen as *too convenient*, particularly since Yılmaz, a refugee from Turkey, had spent

much time in Germany, where he had stayed quite openly and there was never any attempt to charge him with criminal offences . . . [The original intention of Yılmaz, John Austin-Walker and others was] to discuss finding a peaceful solution to the war in Kurdistan and self-determination for the Kurdish people. He [later] said he will not seek judicial review of the Home Secretary's decision, having had his confidence in the British judicial system severely undermined by the courts' passive endorsement of the extradition request. But he will use the German courts as an opportunity to present the case of the Kurdish people and to expose the collaboration of Europe's governments with the Turkish State.[4]

In the AP news item where this extract was taken, mention was made of the German authorities "seeking Öcalan on a 1990 warrant." This refers to the time the German State prosecuted the PKK which up until then was a legal political party. The Turkish State was doing its utmost to have the PKK criminalized throughout Europe as a terrorist organisation. Its deputy chief of staff in 1995 stated "We'll finish terrorism but we are being held back by democracy and human rights."[5] Around that time there had been a horrible massacre "in the village of Geri [when] 30 people, mainly women and children, were brutally killed." This massacre was reported as the work of PKK 'terrorists' and the Turkish authorities "showed video-footage for days to members of the European Parliament," in an attempt to discredit the PKK and to have its leadership outlawed as 'terrorists'. Subsequently a delegation from a human rights association went to the village of Geri itself and came up with somewhat different findings. Members of the delegation "included the President of the now banned Socialist Party" and also Hatip Dicle, "ex-MP of the Democracy Party (DEP), currently serving 15 years imprisonment alongside Leyla Zana and three other DEP MPs."[6] In Dicle's opinion, "shared by all the members of our delegation . . . this massacre was an act of the contra-guerilas." But even though discredited the Turkish State would regard its work of that period as highly successful, given that the German prosecution of the PKK at that period resulted in its being banned. Dicle also makes the point that whenever anything sympathetic to the Kurdish struggle is happening 'on the eve of important international gatherings', the Turkish State will move to undermine and subvert the Kurdish case.

Beşikçi was awaiting trial in a Turkish prison that same year. In an interview with Amnesty International he commented on the German prosecution, that the one thing it did establish was the existence of a 'secret agreement between the NATO alliance and Turkey in relation to Kurdistan.'

The Turkish State resorts to terrorism to achieve or maintain its ends and one large area of Turkey, the southeast, has been under martial law for years. The southeast of Turkey is the northwest of Kurdistan. Kurdish people have been executed summarily in this area for decades. The savagery of the Turkish military has been such that Kurdish people have crossed the Iraqi border. They would rather face Saddam Hussein than the monstrosities of the Turkish military.

During the 1960s there was a strong student movement in Turkey as in different parts of the world and Öcalan emerged from this. The political system of that time has been described as 'democratic fascism'. Even that was too liberal for the military and they conducted a coup in 1971. The young Beşikçi had been doing his own sociological research from the early 1960s, coming up with certain findings in relation to the Kurdish people that did not suit the establishment, academic or political. He was by turn marginalized, victimized, excluded from academic work, had his work censored and suppressed; later he was brought before the law and imprisoned. It is ironic that a couple of the present Turkish government were also rebellious students of the period, to the extent that they were imprisoned.

If Beşikçi was Kurdish and not Turkish he would be dead already. In the western 'democracies' he would neither be imprisoned nor murdered, just marginalized. There are different ways of suppressing the work of writers and it is doubtful if even one country in the world exists where freedom of expression can be taken for granted. Beşikçi's writings are suppressed by the Turkish authorities but people also need to pay attention to the fact that his work is not available to the English-speaking public of the world. None of his 33 books has so far been published in the English language.[7]

There is a block on information about Kurdistan. The UK media are either silent or party to the different forms of propaganda issued on Turkey's behalf. The situation is epitomized by the UK travel industry who, under the nose of HM Government, try to sell us 'Summer Sunshine Holidays' in a war-ravaged police state. The Turkish propaganda is often blatant but masquerading as news, as in the notorious article run by *The Observer* in September 1997, attacking "the PKK in particular and the Kurdish community in general [which] consisted of a series of unsubstantiated allegations ranging from the perverse to the bizarre made by a young Kurd who had either been terrorized or disorientated or compromised by Turkish intelligence." Harold Pinter and Lord Avebury were among those who condemned the newspaper publicly and many people were outraged to discover that such blatant disinformation circulates in one of the top 'quality' newspapers. It was important that *The Observer* should have been condemned but those who were too outraged might be suffering delusions about the UK media; it indicates the depth of untruth to which they have become accustomed.

Of course this is a time when the public receives images of starving children in Africa as adverts for national charities; the images themselves are structured on disinformation, much of it racist. These charities are headed by a vanguard of millionaire celebrities; members of the aristocracy, rock stars and movie stars; 29 football stars, dashing young captains of industry, and so on. In their wake the public is supposed to donate money as a moral duty – or perhaps not quite, the money is to be given on the understanding that the suffering experienced by the starving children has to do with the inherent nature of Africa itself. It has nothing to do with politics, nothing to do with the foreign policy of external forces, not interest rates and not the movement of capital, nothing to do with 'guidelines' that may be enforced by the IMF or the World Bank. None of that. Instead the suffering is to be seen as a sort of physical attribute of the African continent, perhaps of the 'African character'. If the African adult population could learn to plan more efficiently and devise better strategies then they would take better care of their children.

Until that indefinite point in the future the charities of the western democracies have to do the job for them, self determination is not an option, not yet, and YOU can help! Such is the nonsense fed to the British people.

The peculiar relationship the UK media have with the public was in evidence a few weeks ago [26 April], again in *The Observer*; this time it was a feature article by Norman Stone, "renowned Oxford historian". It was little more than a public relations exercise on behalf of the Turkish State. Professor Stone is currently at the Department of International Relations, Bilkent University, Ankara. Stone's views are of the far right variety and he is open in praise of those he describes as the 'true heroes' of our time, e.g. Brian Crozier.[8] For very many years Professor Stone's 'hero' was an "operative of the CIA," and a leading figure "within the whole panoply of right wing . . . intelligence and propaganda agencies" including straight CIA-funded projects such as the Congress for Cultural Freedom and Forum World Features.

Crozier was also a founding member of the secretive but highly influential Pinay Circle, "an international right-wing propaganda group which brings together serving or retired intelligence officers and politicians with links to right-wing intelligence factions from most of the countries in Europe . . ."[9] In the UK he founded the Institute for the Study of Conflict, "part of a network of right wing bodies . . . lecturing on subversion to the British army and the police."[10] This network included Common Cause, the Economic League and *bona fide* agencies of the British State such as MI5, much of whose "intelligence work was inspired not by the demands of security but by extreme right wing political ideas."[11] Another colleague was Brigadier Frank Kitson who in 1969 "was seconded to Oxford University for a year to read and synthesize the literature on counter-insurgency. His thesis was published in 1971 as *Low Intensity Operations*, and a year later he was given command of a brigade in Belfast to test his theories."[12]

Crozier is one of an international group of 'terrorist experts' who argues for "the concept of internal war ... and the parallel ... between the situation of a country at war with an external enemy, and the country faced with a situation like Ulster, or Vietnam, or Turkey or Uruguay." If the general public in these countries can swallow the idea that they are at war then all kinds of 'emergency regulations' can be introduced.[13] As with Professor Stone he is an apologist for the brutalities of the Turkish military. 1971 was a crucial period in recent Turkish-Kurdish history, "when the army overthrew the Demirel government ... and thousands of people were arrested and tortured in counter-insurgency centres which had been set up by Turkish officers trained by the US in Panama."[14] This is interpreted by Crozier as a "military intervention to force the creation of a government determined to restore order." In response to an article critical of "allegations of ill-treatment during interrogation in Ulster" he wonders why people were "so distressed [by such] relative mildness ... What if it [had extended] to the grim horrors reported during ... the early 1970s in Turkey?"[15] Then he justifies the barbarism of the Turkish State Security forces on the grounds that it "undoubtedly helped to provide the security forces with the intelligence they needed [to smash the Turkish People's Liberation Army] as an effective instrument of revolution."

I think if I was Kurdish I would have become a wee bit tired hearing European writers and others urging the Turkish State to change its ways. It is difficult to think of one country in Europe that does not collude with Turkish ruling authority in one way or another. 'Turkish ruling authority' is just another name for Turkish National Security which is just another name for the Turkish military. Beyond *The Observer* and the mainstream media in general the contempt for the UK public is in evidence elsewhere, including at the highest levels of Government as when the previously discredited academic, Professor Paul Wilkinson, was commissioned by Lord Lloyd "to provide 'an academic view as to the nature of the terrorist threat.'"

It would be of more value to the people of Kurdistan that we let our own governments know that we are aware of the reality, that we know what is happening behind the closed doors of power, we know of the cowardice of our own politicians and academics, and of their complicity, both at the present time and historically. We should accept responsibility and challenge those who hide in the shadows. If we expect media coverage of this 'dirty war' and the atrocities being perpetrated against the Kurdish people we do so in the knowledge that weapons and torture implements used by the Turkish State are supplied by the Scottish and British business community, as well as those of the USA, Germany and France.

While Professor Stone praises Turkey as the "fastest-growing economy in the European region" another academic has now spent nearly 15 years of his life in prison. Beşikçi is being punished as an example to other writers, to other activists, to other academics, to other sociologists, to other scientists and – most crucially – to other Turks. During one trial speech he made the basic point that it was not he who was on trial but science itself. How can the science of sociology exist as a valid field of study until he is released from prison and his work made freely available? Until then the entire subject is contaminated, not only in Turkey and in Kurdistan but elsewhere throughout the world.

(2001)

# Solidarity with İsmail Beşikçi

*Left to right are James Kelman, Bernard MacLaverty*
*and Kurdish musicians, including Newroz.*

By 1997 Dr İsmail Beşikçi had spent nearly 15 years of his life in prison. Each time an essay, book or booklet of his was printed he was given a further term and so far the aggregate stood at more than 100 years. Under Turkish law his publisher was prosecuted simultaneously and to date has received sentences in the region of 14 years. At one stage less than two years ago the two men "were abused [and] physically assaulted while being conducted from prison to the court … [and their] documents … rendered useless." In 1998 James Kelman's collection of stories, *The Good Times*, was published and the launch took place in Glasgow and Edinburgh in 'solidarity with the Freedom for İsmail Beşikçi campaign'.

*Above left Neville Lawrence, father of Stephen Lawrence, and central figure in the Stephen Lawrence family campaign for justice, spoke alongside Suresh Grover of the Monitoring Group and the National Council for Civil Liberties.*

For these events in Edinburgh and Glasgow Beşikçi's publisher, Ünsal Öztürk, made the trip from Turkey. He is seen here in a Glasgow cafe with Kelman, Neville Lawrence, and translator Firat Erbil.

(1998)

# The University of Strathclyde Students' Association Grants Honorary Life Membership to Kurdish Leader, Abdullah Öcalan

Bestowing an honour such as this makes it not just a meeting but a special occasion. It is marvellous that the students of Strathclyde University should honour Abdullah Öcalan in this way. As former students here, both myself and my wife Marie, I am very pleased personally to see it happen.

Of course I am also aware of the pitfalls in honouring one individual in this way. It could tie us into that notion of 'The Great Leader', the one without whom we would all be Lost. I find such a notion not only unacceptable, I find it repugnant. People here will feel the same. But there are those who fall for it and there are those in whose interest it is to enforce the falsification.

And what a terrible disservice it does to those hundreds of thousands of courageous Kurdish people who have fought and died in the struggle toward liberation, toward self determination. Those who are opposed to a people's right to self determination will use any means at their disposal to under-cut and oppose that struggle. A typical method is to transform the liberation movement into the political project of one tiny group of foreign extremist fanatics. Ringleaders! The Vanguard! Without these ringleaders and vanguards the masses would be content to know their own place in the scheme of things, be content with their lot and a belief system grounded in the hereafter, looking forward to a glorious Life after Death, if they are religious, and the docile masses are always portrayed as religious. In the case of Kurdistan it gives the idea that these millions of people are a nomadic lumpen proletariat who would be content to chase goats up and down mountains, ignorant of their own history, living in abject poverty, kow-towing to their political and cultural superiors, if it wasn't for these foreign left-wing infiltrators who are all atheists and communists.

Even better when the authorities can lay the blame for the discontent on the shoulders of one individual. It is a strategy used by corrupt rulers to cling onto power. They strive to establish that there is no liberation movement without the Great Leader. No mass struggle, only the Great Leader.

Once the ruling authorities and their allies have this established their chore is straightforward. To destabilize the struggle they need only 'expose' the Great Leader. They transform the Great Leader into a greedy and power-hungry charlatan whose overriding impulse is self-interest and self-glorification. Ruling authority will use their propaganda 'to reveal' the Great Leader as a contemptible coward who enters into acts of betrayals with all and sundry to achieve his own evil end. They will lie and distort the truth to portray the Great Leader as a weak and selfish coward who has sold out his closest comrades in a last ditch attempt to save his own skin.

This is not to say that greedy and self-glorifying Great Leaders do not exist. Of course they do. Typically we find that most such individuals are not really leaders at all, they are tyrants; placed into power by the so-called western democracies. This has been the case in Europe, Asia, Africa, Australasia and the Americas. It is a strategy we associate with imperialism. These so-called Great Leaders lead no movement at all. What they have is a paid army, a fascist administration, and the financial, material and human resources of these same western democracies. This has been the case in both Iran and Iraq and an example is the Shah of Iran.

The Turkish authorities want to reach a position where they can say: if not for Öcalan there would be no Kurdish liberation movement. It is only through his evil machinations that such a thing exists at all. This is not just a lie it is an offensive lie and it dishonours the Kurdish people. Those who make use of the lie are engaged in destabilizing the liberation movement. And this is the context to which we should pay heed when we hear these dark rumours about Öcalan doing secret deals that will sell out his Kurdish Workers' Party (PKK) comrades, compromise the liberation struggle, and deal a death blow to the birthright of the Kurdish people.

These dirty tricks and double-dealings are predictable and people should be strong enough to treat them with contempt. It happens during periods of negotiation. The ruling authority who holds power will undermine any bargaining counter from the other side. It is quite simple. They refuse to negotiate until they have absolutely no choice. They will drag out the process for as long as they can. The Turkish State is being dragged to the negotiating table and they do not like it one bit. Thus they will postpone it and postpone it and postpone it for as long as it takes and for as long as they can, in the hope that it all blows over and is forgotten about. Nobody cares about the long term. It is basic: those who hold power will cling onto power.

The question of Kurdish liberation and the exercise of self determination is very complex. A look at maps of the Middle East will give some idea of the complexity. A highly unusual thing occurs in an old one I have of the Middle East. There is an entity that is Kurdistan. Now to carry such a map in Turkey before 2002 was a criminal offence. Yes! Even to carry the map! The name Kurdistan was against the law. Even to utter the word: Kurdistan! – a criminal offence. To sing a Kurdish song: a criminal offence. To give your children a Kurdish name: a criminal offence. In Turkey to use the Kurdish language in any way at all was a criminal offence. The Turkish authorities jailed Kurdish people, they tortured Kurdish people and they put Kurdish people to death because they refused to lie down and accept such iniquitous and anti-human legislation.

The juridical system in Turkey may be complex but its central purpose is straightforward, it sanctifies the state and protects it from the people. The Constitution entered existence in November of 1982. The very possibility of democracy was denied. This from the opening preamble:

> no thought or impulse [may be cherished] against Turkish national interests, against the existence of Turkey, against the principle of the indivisibility of the state and its territory, against the historical and moral values of Turkishness, against

nationalism as defined by [Mustafa Kemal] Atatürk, against
his principles, reforms and civilizing efforts . . .

Mustafa Kemal Atatürk was the major Turkish figure of
the First World War period. The struggle for the liberation
of Kurdistan returns us to the end of the First World War
when the deals were being done, when the land spoils and
plunder were being divvied up by the Allies and when
Turkey, given the okay by Britain and America, cheated the
Kurdish people out of their right to nationhood. Whether or
not nationhood is, ultimately, a good or a bad thing is not
the concern. The issue is that at the end of the First World
War nation status was on the cards and it was denied.
Kurdistan was partitioned, the land divided between the
surrounding countries: Turkey, Syria, Iraq and Iran, and it
happened to the benefit of foreign interests, led by the UK,
by France and by the USA.

The annexation of Kurdistan, the attempted genocide and
the continued oppression of the Kurdish people are three of
the major scandals of this century; a fourth was the genocide
in Armenia. The British State has had a pivotal role. During
the 1920s Britain needed a client-state "to secure [British
capital's] right to exploit the oilfields of Southern Kurdistan."
What did they do? Basically they created a country, gave it a
king, and called it Iraq. Britain has continued to collude in the
terrorist assaults on the Kurdish people from then until the
present. The British State has held great influence and could
have tried to aid the cause of justice. They have never done
so. But why should anyone be surprised by that? There is no
place for such naivety. We have to pass beyond a position that

confuses the procedures of state with a value-system centred on ethical standards and moral principles.

Abdullah Öcalan wasn't born until after the end of the Second World War. He is of my own generation. In fact he is two years younger than me. Fifty years ago during our teens and early twenties it was a very different time. Public protest was common. The Vietnam War raged in all its horror. Liberation struggles were taking place in different parts of the world; class struggles and pan-nationalist struggles. Within the western democracies themselves such things were happening. But there was a heavy reaction to that and assaults on freedom took place in most every region of the world.

Back then there was a sense of solidarity that nowadays seems from another world. It even spread across class lines. Middle class students engaged, and many academics also engaged, and some were jailed for their part in "fomenting student unrest" – as though the students were incapable of their own "unrest". There was a very strong student move-ment also in Turkey during the mid to late 1960s and Öcalan emerged from this. The political system in Turkey at that time has been described as 'democratic fascism', although even that was too liberal for the Turkish military who conducted another coup in 1971.

People may see the award of this honour to Öcalan as symbolic. Fair enough. Öcalan may well be a symbol for millions of people but first and foremost he is a living, breathing human being who has been locked up in a Turkish prison since 1999. It was a very difficult period. Öcalan had been in Syria where he had lived on the run for a long number of years. Until he was betrayed by the usual suspects, the so-called western democracies: Britain, America, Italy, Germany and so on.

Then, as now, there was a media block on information about the situation in Kurdistan. The British media were either silent or party to the different forms of propaganda issued on Turkey's behalf. Turkish State propaganda is often so blatant it is laughable yet news agencies allow it to run as though unimpeachable. The situation was epitomized by the UK travel industry who, under the nose of H.M. Government, sold the British people 'Summer Sunshine Holidays' in a war-ravaged police state. One notorious article run by *The Observer* newspaper in September 1997, attacked "the PKK in particular and the Kurdish community in general [which] consisted of a series of unsubstantiated allegations ranging from the perverse to the bizarre made by a young Kurd who had either been terrorized or disorientated or compromised by Turkish intelligence."

People were outraged to discover that such blatant disinformation circulates in one of the top 'quality' newspapers. Of course it was important to condemn *The Observer* but those who were too outraged might have been suffering delusions about the British media. What were they expecting, honesty, truth and justice?

Until his capture in Italy Abdullah Öcalan was one of the most wanted men in the world. But how did that happen? Only a few years before he was simply a high profile Kurdish politician, founder member and President of the PKK. How did he get from there to being such a monstrous criminal?

In the first report I read of his capture the pro-Turkey bias was blatant. From Associated Press one comment stood out, that there have been "no executions in Turkey since 1984." This was a disgraceful distortion of the truth. Who knows the number of executions committed in that country since 1984. What we have had there are summary executions.

In the same Associated Press news item much was made of the German authorities "seeking Abdullah Öcalan on a 1990 warrant." Up until then the PKK was a legitimate political party. Meantime the Turkish State was doing its utmost to have this political party criminalized as a terrorist organisation. This was consistent with their own 1982 Constitution where it was a crime even to use the word Kurdistan. This was a period in the recent past where young Kurdish people and their Turkish comrades were being imprisoned for daring the authorities by unfurling Kurdish flags in the law courts, and by singing Kurdish songs.

What these young people were witnessing was the criminalisation of the entire Kurdish people. Once criminalisation is 'allowed' anything is possible; barbarism, mass murder, genocide. Once a political party is outlawed it means anything at all except dialogue and negotiation. People are ignored, ghettoized, marginalized; jailed, tortured and killed. There are no rules, and no mercy. Who cares what happens to a bunch of 'terrorists', never mind that up until the day before they were a community of women and men who advocated a particular politics and way ahead for their culture and community.

I mentioned elsewhere how back in 1995 "in the village of Geri 30 people, mainly women and children were brutally killed." This massacre was reported as the work of PKK 'terrorists' and the Turkish authorities 'showed video footage for days to members of the European Parliament, 'in an attempt to discredit the PKK and to have its leadership outlawed as 'terrorists'. Subsequently a delegation from a Human Rights Association went to the village of Geri itself and came up with a different finding, "shared by all the members of our delegation . . . this massacre was an act of the contra-guerrillas."

But even though discredited the Turkish State propaganda worked; the German prosecution of the PKK resulted in it being banned as an illegal organisation. The Turkish State humiliated the European Parliament by serving them a complete fabrication about the PKK. In fact they themselves may well have held ultimate responsibility for the massacre.

While awaiting trial in a Turkish prison during that period the great Turkish sociologist İsmail Beşikçi was interviewed by Amnesty International and commented on the German prosecution of the PKK. He said that the one thing it did establish was the existence of a "secret agreement between the NATO alliance and Turkey in relation to Kurdistan."

In 1953 Dr Mohammad Mosaddeq headed the government in Iran. Mosaddeq was detested by the Turkish, US and the British states. One of his most blatant criminal acts was to put a check on monarchy and ruling authority by making it subject to the democratic control of the Iranian people. A similar plan was suggested 400 years earlier, in 16th-century Scotland, by the writer George Buchanan. He argued that all monarchs should be subject to democratic control and that none should exercise an absolute God-given authority.

In 16th-century Scotland this was anathema to the monarchy and the financial interests of the ruling class. So too in

20th-century Iran the financial and business interests of the ruling class were endangered by these dangerous notions of democratic control. The British State acted quickly along-side the USA to get rid of the danger by destabilizing the government, criminalising and occasionally assassinating intellectuals and activists. Mosaddeq was captured, imprisoned and detained under house-arrest until his death in 1967. Thus he avoided execution. But no ruling authority wants to create a martyr; perhaps a factor in why Abdullah Öcalan remains alive.

Britain and America installed their own Great Leader in Iran: the Shah. By means of the terrorism he practised on the Iranian people, aided and abetted by Britain and the USA, the Shah managed "to hold onto Iran" for the next 25 years, acting on behalf of the so-called Western democracies, who themselves were acting on behalf of global financial and business interests. The revolution that ousted the Shah brought to power an Islamic republic headed by Ayatollah Khomeini.

During the 25 years of absolute rule by the Shah one place of freedom was the mosque. A general problem for tyrannies and dictatorships is religion and the problems effected by religious belief and belief systems. It is difficult to attack religious institutions at fundamental levels and virtually impossible to criminalize entire religions, although down through the centuries both have been tried by ruling authorities.

In some societies it is the only indoor public space left. Across Kurdistan restrictions on freedom of movement have existed in one place or another for decades while in Turkey martial law has been established on many occasions. Places of religious worship are all-important within tyrannies and dictatorships, not just for expressions of religious faith but as meeting places. People chat to one another. It happens in mosques, churches, temples and synagogues.

While the Shah ruled there was a powerful irony at play for the Kurdish peoples. In their efforts to contain the Kurdish population in Iran the State's propaganda unit broadcast Kurdish programmes in Kurmanji, the Kurdish language. It didn't matter that this was right-wing pro-authoritarian propaganda, the crucial factor was that it took place in the Kurds' own language. Kurdish people could listen and hear their language in this public arena; traditional Kurdish songs, snippets of Kurdish history: what an extraordinary experience.

I mentioned earlier the inaugural Freedom of Expression event in Istanbul in 1997. Perhaps there should be room for another event, The Freedom to Know. This event could deal with our ignorance of our own history, the denial of our right to learn where we are, who we are, who we were, where we were; to know the stories, languages, songs and traditions of our own people.

It is very hard for people to determine their own existence when they don't even know who they are nor to which communities, groups and even families they might belong.

Abdullah Öcalan has spent most of his life either on the run or in prison. He and others are arguing in favour of a different way ahead taking into account the most awkward questions, including the relationship of armed warfare to the liberation movement, and the place of the nation state in regard to self determination in the 21st century. If I read this correctly this vision is anti-state and validates ideas on group and community autonomy. I approve of that! Fascism attacks communities and leaves us stranded as individuals, attempting to make sense of the world in the most isolated manner.

Kurdish history, as with Scottish history, belongs to radical history, like that of any marginalized people or community. It is suppressed as a matter of course. The people of Kurdistan have been struggling for decades for the right to determine their own existence. This honour that Strathclyde students are paying to Abdullah Öcalan represents more than an honour to one individual, it recognizes the justice of the struggle. From Scotland the message is one of support and solidarity. Let the politicians in this country heed the students.

(21 June 2015)

# But What Is It They Are
# Trying To Express?

I need to say that the views I express here are my own, derived from my own perception; the result of my own reading, my own knowledge and my own observations and if I go wrong I apologise in advance. This evening is entitled Remembering Turkish Voices of Dissent.[1] I see a need to take this a step beyond if we are to come to terms with what is happening in Turkey, and most especially in the southeast, Turkish-Kurdistan, not only at present but for several generations. To describe the 'voices of dissent' as Turkish is something I can only do with major qualification. I have to make reference to Kurdistan and the plight of the Kurdish people. If not then the danger is that we miss the most fundamental factors. When we say 'Turkish voices' do we mean to include Kurdish voices? If we say, 'yes, of course', then we may have fallen into a trap, that we allowed the Turkish State to set the agenda, that the name Turkish embraces Kurds.

Oppression in Turkey goes through periods of severity, then tails off. For the past couple of years it's been nightmarish. People here will have followed events and be familiar with the name of another writer now imprisoned, Gültan Kışanak. She is also co-mayor of Diyarbakır which is the main city in Turkish-Kurdistan. "[A]fter months of armed conflict in the city center that ended in March 2016 ... [she and her male co-mayor] Fırat Anlı were detained by Turkish police on 25 October 2016 ... Just after the detention, the internet connection across the Kurdish region was cut. As of 27 October 2016, millions of people still have no internet access. This blackout attempt aims at silencing the voice of people in the region as well as to prevent them from exercising their right to be informed about developments."

Kışanak has been an activist all her life:

> In the 1980s [I] was imprisoned ... in notoriously brutal conditions, with torture and killings. To be Kurdish, to be a woman and to be leftist created triple difficulties for me. I was kept in a dog kennel for six months because I refused to say "I am not a Kurd but a Turk". Our older women friends, our mothers' age were tortured because they could not speak Turkish. I still have signs of torture from those days on my body.

What we have to understand is that the Turkish State has done all in its power to convince the world, including its own population, that there is no such thing as Kurdistan, no such people as Kurdish people, no such culture, no such language, no such anything; nothing. The Turkish State has attempted to extirpate every last vestige of Kurdishness, and put into its place Turkishness. The Turkish State would discuss Turkish voices of dissent forever and ever, but if we exchange Turkish for Kurdish, it's another story.

A deal was done at the end of the First World War between the major western powers. Kurdistan was divided into four, and became part of Turkey, Iraq, Syria and Iran. For almost a hundred years now these millions of Kurdish people have been without a country, and for many of them it's been a form of hell on earth. But from the ashes of that the Kurdish people have refused to die out, they have refused to become extinct. It is estimated that there are twenty million Kurdish people in Turkey, add another twenty million in the Middle East and Europe.

Much of the campaigning material I see about the current situation connects directly with Freedom of Speech and Expression but when campaigns stop and start on Freedom of Speech and Expression, I am not **necessarily** sympathetic. Also, I don't see arrests and imprisonments in Turkey as 'arbitrary' at all. I think we need to be very cautious on that one.

Nor has it much to do with general principles concerning Freedom of Speech and Expression. It is a mistake to insist that it is about general principles. When you do this you fail to take into account the reality of the Turkish Constitution, and the Turkish Penal Code. These are not ethical issues. The far-right in Turkey which is bringing its own pressure on Erdoğan and the Turkish Government has a very solid foundation within the Turkish legal profession. These people are lawyers by profession. General principles don't apply. They don't give two hoots about general principles. What matters is what exists in the constitution and how best that can be applied in civil society. In other words what they can get away with, and they will push that as far as it goes, and when that fails the lawyers and the rest of them will step aside and leave it to the military. That's what happens. I'm not a lawyer and

I'm not a soldier. I'm making general observations based on my own understanding.

I once wrote **against** a campaign which concerned Freedom of Speech and Expression, or at least it so appeared. I didn't see it as that at all. I just thought it was an elitist kind of thing, at best silly, but essentially crap. It laboured under the misapprehension that here in the UK we have a long tradition of freedom of speech and expression which is inviolable and that we should do all in our power to maintain these freedoms against the forces of ignorance. I beg your pardon? What a joke. One point I tried to make was that it was ludicrous to say that freedom of speech and expression existed in the UK. I also said that when you attack people don't be surprised when they attack ye back. Self Defence is No Offence.

English literature attacks all sorts of people, and this is a general rule if not principle. English literature is the expression of a value-system. If a writer fails to challenge values within this system then he or she is guilty. Guilty of what? Guilty of failing to challenge these values. Which values? You tell me. Are there values in this society that we should attack? Come on, I'm talking to you writers. Are there any values that we cannot help but attack in order to write honestly, and truthfully?

Freedom of Speech and Expression. Freedom to speak about what? Freedom to express yourself about what?

Forget the general principle. To see this as a general principle plays into the hands of despots, dictatorships, and every other authoritarian regime.

They don't give a damn about Freedom of Speech and Expression. It is irrelevant. They already have Freedom of

Speech and Expression. Even better: they have freedom of action. They say and do what they like. Right is might. They have the power and they have the might.

And they will let us say and do what we like, as long as they don't disapprove.

What is it that the Turkish State is trying to stop people saying, or thinking, or expressing? This meeting is also in support of Aslı Erdoğan, and to demonstrate solidarity with her. Aslı Erdoğan is not Kurdish, but Turkish. İsmail Beşikçi, sociologist, anthropologist, historian spent 17 years of his life in prison. Why? Why are so many journalists and writers and artists and trades union organizers and politicians and members of the judiciary, and every kind of people you care to mention languishing in prison right now?

It has nothing to do with general principles of Freedom of Speech and Expression. It has everything to do with speaking on behalf of Kurdish people, of expressing our horror and condemnation of the Turkish State's barbaric assaults on Kurdish people. Speaking freely on the situation in Kurdistan is to break the law, not to breach a principle of natural justice.

Aslı Erdoğan is in prison for her support of the Kurdish people, for the fact of her solidarity and where this has taken her, like many other heroic and courageous Turkish people. Some are Christian, some are Muslim; some hold other religions, some are atheists. In common is their humanity, their hatred of injustice; their inability to stand aside and pretend they don't see what is happening.

In Turkey in the great majority of cases it is not so much Freedom of Speech and Expression that is the problem, it is speaking on behalf of Kurdish people, it is expressing your horror and absolute condemnation of the Turkish State's soul-destroying inhumanity. I am arguing that speaking freely on the situation in Kurdistan is to break the law, not breach a principle.

When we look at the Turkish Constitution we see that by using certain elements of language we are breaking the law, and there is no freedom enshrined in any place in the world that allows us to break the law. This is part of the difficulty in talking about campaigns concerning so-called Freedom of Speech and Expression. They aren't worth a damn when they come up against State laws. These campaigns on behalf of Turkish writers and issues around Freedom of Expression are crucial, I'm not saying they are not important. Of course they are. But they only take us so far.

It is not freedom of expression that matters so much as the subject matter. I want to shout out my support and my solidarity with the Kurdish people, those people who have been carrying a life or death struggle for decades.

It doesn't matter if the Turkish State 'grants' me the Freedom to Express my solidarity. I have to grab that opportunity when I can, with or without any concessions. Freedom is not a concession. Am I supposed to request of a brutal dictator that he grants me Freedom of Speech and Expression? It is ludicrous.

Courageous Turkish people must be supported but the **reasons** why they are being punished must also be supported. We cannot support Turkish dissidents blindly. We cannot conduct campaigns on their behalf and ignore why it is they are in that horrendous position.

There is a war going on in Turkey. I'm not 100% surprised if people in this room don't know about this. The UK and most of the Western so-called democracies are either cowed into silence by Turkey, or find it in their interests to remain silent. "There is a media block on information about the situation in Kurdistan. Our media are either silent or party to the different forms of propaganda issued on Turkey's behalf. Turkish State propaganda is often so blatant it is laughable yet news agencies allow it to run as though unimpeachable."

Here now are words by Gültan Kışanak:

In the 1990s there was no sign of freedom – just like now – I worked for newspapers where Kurdish and women's rights were the main issue. These were alternatives to the mainstream newspapers. The conditions for journalists, especially for Kurdish journalists were harsh – just like today. Some of our journalist friends were killed while they were doing their work. I worked as a journalist for 13 years and published sections focusing on women's issues within the newspaper.

After 2007, women became more visible and powerful. The 2007 elections were revolutionary for both Kurdish and Turkish women. Eight out of 26 Kurdish MPs were women. Women became more confident as co-chairs and men had to accept them as equals. Other political parties were embarrassed and started to introduce a co-chair system as well.

The state's military operations in the Kurdish regions during the last year have destroyed all city life. The Turkish Human Rights Organisation has published a report about what has happened between 16 August 2015 and 18 March 2016 in seven cities and 22 towns in the Kurdish regions. A total of one million and 642 thousand people were affected by the state's operations and curfews. 320 people have lost their lives (72 children and 62 women). Tens of thousands of houses were destroyed. At least 250 thousand people are homeless now. Women and children have been especially affected by this damage. Most now living in uncivilized conditions in tents without water and electricity for months. They cannot find enough food and clean water to keep them alive. They don't have access to any health system. Although women have tried to protect themselves and their children from illnesses, the rates of premature birth, neonatal deaths, stillbirth, and child deaths have all increased. Children are traumatized and most have lost their normal lives and trust.

[About the coup in July this year] we can see that the high ranking military generals and personnel who carried out a very brutal war against Kurdish people were directly involved . . . these [same] generals, who have carried out crimes against Kurds and violated all human rights in Kurdistan, are **not** blamed for this reason. They are only blamed for [their failed] coup attempt . . . the generals who organized the coup, are claiming the significant role they played in the war against Kurds as part of their defence. They try to justify themselves by proclaiming what big Turkish nationalists they are.

After the coup Erdoğan started a dialogue with most of the opposition political parties [but excluded] the HDP . . .

Some of you will know of the Peoples' Democratic Party (HDP), "the pro-Kurdish Peoples' Party which is the third largest party in Turkey." This party has been operational for less than two years in which time it has gone on to unite different people, groups, communities and the Turkish left. For HDP "the first step is the establishment of democratic and autonomous local governments." Ayla Akat Ata, another women's rights activist now in prison has explained that

> From the beginning, the Kurdish movement has had three main aims: national struggle, class struggle and gender struggle. All ... three are as important as each other if we are to find a real solution for our people ... The Kurds will create a democratic autonomous system against the centralist, barbaric and corrupt state system. To create something better for people might not be easy, but Kurds will succeed and this will benefit Turkey and the entire Middle East. We want to create a strong parliamentary system with more power given to the regions. The existence of a one-man system of rule is destroying the democratic legitimacy of parliament and has significantly weakened it ... [It] doesn't matter how many elections you have, democracy is merely reduced to a rubber stamp for dictatorship. Sadly a Turkish nationalist block exists and supports this type of dictatorial rule.

There is one essential campaign that we might wage, for the release to freedom of a man who, with others, has been trying to work out a way to resolve the situation, that might bring a meaningful way ahead for Kurdish people, and not only in Turkey but in Syria and Iraq, and Iran too. This man has spent the last few years working his ideas out on the page and for a brief period he was in direct negotiation with the Turkish Government. I refer to Abdullah Öcalan. We might begin by requesting that Mister Erdoğan and the Turkish government **resume** negotiations with Mr Öcalan and other Kurdish politicians – yes, resume, even while he was in prison he and senior Kurdish politicians were talking together, but that came to an abrupt end roundabout 2012.

You must surely be aware that Öcalan has been imprisoned since 1999. He lived on the run for a long number of years, until betrayed by the usual suspects: Britain, America, Italy and Germany. He was one of the most wanted men in the world. How come? Only a few years before he was simply a high profile Kurdish politician, a founder member and President of the Kurdish Workers' Party (PKK). How did he get from there to being such a monstrous criminal? In the first report I read of his capture the pro-Turkey bias was blatant. From Associated Press one comment stood out, that there have been "no executions in Turkey since 1984." This was a disgraceful distortion of the truth. Who knows the number of executions committed in that country since 1984. What we have had there are summary executions. In the same news item was a reference to the German authorities "seeking Abdullah Öcalan on a 1990 warrant." Up until then the PKK was a legitimate political party. The Turkish State had done its utmost to have this political party criminalized as a terrorist organisation.

And it succeeded. Once criminalisation is 'allowed' anything is possible. There are no rules, no mercy. People are ignored, ghettoized, marginalized; jailed, tortured, killed. Who cares what happens to a bunch of 'terrorists', never mind that up until the day before they were a community of women and men who advocated a particular politics and way ahead for their culture and native lands.

It doesn't matter if the Turkish State 'grants' me the Freedom to Express my solidarity. I have to grab that opportunity when I can, with or without any concessions. Freedom is not a concession. Am I supposed to request of a brutal dictator that he grants me Freedom of Speech and Expression? It is ludicrous.

PEN International can begin by offering our support and solidarity with Kurdish writers and artists, and sending a strong message of support and solidarity to the Kurdish PEN Centre, if it hasn't been bombed out of existence already. The last I heard it had been broken into and ransacked.

(2016)

# Who's Kidding Who?[1]

People who donate to charitable bodies and other formations associated with human rights and humanitarian issues, e.g. Amnesty International, PEN International, Medical Aid to Palestine should engage in a little more study. There is no need to submerge oneself in the colonial history of the British Empire, nor of the other 'powers'. Only be aware that in such matters as 'upholding democratic principles' people from overseas may feel they hold an advantage over the populations of England, Wales, Scotland and the north of Ireland. Members of the British electorate who concern themselves with the reality of the oppression and suffering within Turkey and who charge President Recep Tayyip Erdoğan and the Turkish State to pay heed to humanitarian examples and democratic principles, should prepare for the likely retort: who's kidding who?

The diverse peoples of the defeated Ottoman Empire were well aware of the historical reality, rather than the imaginative take on it created by the cultural wing of the British State. They knew that the

French and British reached a secret agreement in 1916 (Sykes-Picot Agreement) dividing Mesopotamia into zones of British

93

and French influence. This division of spoils included a share for Tsarist Russia. A proclamation was issued shortly after British troops captured Baghdad in 1917. "Our armies do not come into your cities and lands as conquerors or enemies, but as liberators . . . You are free to participate in your own civil affairs . . . in collaboration with the political representatives of Britain who accompany the Army."[2] Then they imposed colonial rule, ignored the secret agreement and seized the oil-rich province.[3]

The founder of modern Turkey, Mustafa Kemal Atatürk, created an opposition party based on his knowledge of how mainstream politics operate in England and Great Britain as a whole. This was the late 1920s. It was not a serious enterprise. There again, he knew the reality of the British system. This is how one of his biographers put it: Kemal "had studied the English [political] system and approved of it." As far as the public is concerned the political parties are forever "attacking each other", but this only happens within "office hours": "out of office hours they must be best of friends [and] should dine together in all friendliness . . . working for the good of [England]".[4]

This was the late 1920s. Kemal was dictator at that period and his creation of an 'opposition party' was not farcical, it was designed deliberately and

was not for any kind of libertarian or democratic purpose, he did it to teach his politicians a lesson, that he alone was in charge. [But] it didn't work. Turkish officialdom couldn't cope. They saw their duty to silence all opposition. Even a pretend opposition was too much![5]

Ironically, an authentic opposition grew and developed within Turkey. Diverse communities and formations took their lead from the pretend opposition. They entered the fray properly, authentically: "Government officials were ... driven out of villages; religious leaders were aiding and abetting the groundswell, threats [came] in Armenia; the Kurds were fighting fiercely [and] had invented the Blind Man's Court Martial before [which] every Turk captured was summarily tried and brutally mutilated."[6]

This was too much. Kemal sent in the army. "Martial law was declared, censorship reimposed, newspaper editors punished severely [and] the Turkish troops retaliated cruelly on the Kurds, hanging and imprisoning the leaders, crushing revolt, ejecting every Armenian possible, wiping up the Communists, hanging those who had plotted against him, arrested, bastinadoed and imprisoned a thousand Turks, hung twenty eight of their leaders. The frontiers were cleared, the revolts crushed. Every class, every man and woman – felt and knew the master's hand ..."[7]

That was in 1932. The cry became one of purity and national unity: Turkey for the Turk. This has led to a political system we equate with fascism. And surely this was inevitable from the point Kemal changed

the Arabic characters of Turkish into Latin to revolutionize all thought in Turkey, all Turkish literature, the whole system of written communication between Turk and Turk ... The Koran and New Testament were translated into Turkish ... All prayers in the mosques [had to] be in Turkish. Foreign schools [are] discouraged [and] must omit all reference to religion.

Teachers must teach Turkish . . . The language [is] full of foreign words, Arabic and Persian [must] be eliminated. Tartar [is] the basic language. Tartar words and phrases must be discovered out of old books, documents and songs, revived and used to replace the foreign words. [Then he] called in European experts . . . adopted the German Commercial [Code], the Italian Penal [Code] and the Swiss Civil Code . . . [8]

Nevertheless, it is essential that people from beyond the sphere of Turkish influence gain some understanding of Kemal Atatürk's historical position and why the legacy of Kemalism will continue to command respect from within the country itself. British people who seek to show solidarity with the people of Kurdistan and in the process promote forms of secular, non-authoritarian democracies should compare their present-day situation. In Turkey one hundred years ago Mustafa Kemal Atatürk

changed a monarchy into a republic, reduced an empire to a country, made a religious State into a lay republic, ejected the Sultan, the Caliph, [then] set out to change the whole mentality of the people – their old ideas, their habits, their dress, manners, customs, ways of talking . . . All the arts must be modernized. For four hundred years the priests had forbidden all delineation of the human form . . . [Kemal] opened a mixed school in Ankara to study the nude . . . encouraged women to shed their veils and come out into the open, made them members of his political party with equal footing with men, helped them become doctors and lawyers; two became judges, four elected to the municipal council [and] produced the Children's Bill, regulating the employment of children, forbidding them to be taken to bars, cafes-chantants and uncontrolled cinemas.[9]

"Religion . . . was clogging the machinery of the State . . ." Kemal took it on, he "closed the monasteries, dissolved their organisations . . . destroyed the whole religious basis, the old laws and social life . . .

[He] revolutionized the status of the family and the rights of ownership, forbade polygamy and the harem. [He] radically adjusted the position of women, who ceased to be chattels owned by their husbands [and] became individuals and free citizens . . . [He] forced both parties to a marriage to produce clean bills of health before they could marry . . . introduced the metric system and Gregorian calendar . . . [T]he saluting of superiors and the acknowledgment of salutes by inferiors were changed. The salaam was forbidden . . . [and] the handshake . . . [replaced] the old triple obeisance . . . [and he] made it a punishable offence to laugh at the mad, eccentric or crippled.[10]

The demographic nature of the imprisoned population cannot be ignored. When I was writing this, dated 13 November 2018: "the number of detained and convicted students in Turkey [was] around 70,000." Seventy thousand students. How many of these are Turkish? How many are Kurdish? And how many have no association whatsoever with Kurdistan or Kurdishness?

It was only after the break-up of the Ottoman empire that nation-states came into existence. Prior to then were different societies, different cultures, different political systems: Turks, Kurds, Arabs, Persians, Azerbaijanis, Assyrians, Iraqis and others. And the 'powers' were in at the kill, grabbing what they could. In those days Winston Churchill was not the romantic superhero of contemporary times, the one British children are taught on pain of retribution to love, honour and revere; this brave, upper-class Englishman who won the Second World War all on his own. He was a war-mongering cabinet minister who

> saw Iraq as an experiment in high-technology colonial control. In response to Iraqi resistance, including a country-wide uprising British forces pacified the country using airplanes, armoured cars, firebombs and mustard gas. Air attacks were used to shock and awe, to teach obedience and to force the collection of taxes.[11]

Churchill's utter disregard for the men, women and children of the civilian population, made "officials in London" uneasy. Unlike Churchill they "sometimes had qualms about the violence." But other "colonial administrators expressed enthusiasm for the power of the military enterprise," including Gertrude Bell, "sole woman at the British top table wrangling over the future of the Middle East [and] instrumental in the creation of modern Iraq." The BBC allows Ms Bell a most positive if not unimpeachable salute. Although her "involvement has been debated ever since [what] isn't questioned is her love of the Arab people and their culture. She set up a museum to house some of Iraq's cultural treasures – it is still there today; now known as the National Museum of Iraq."[12]

This is classic Brit-speak, part of the 'two-sides-to-every-story' claptrap, the BBC creates on a daily basis on behalf of the British State. Here we are asked to ignore Gertrude Bell's admiration of the cynical barbarism practised by Churchill and the British military forces on behalf of British capital, and forget that the supreme goal was to steal and secure for British-based capital 'the oil-rich provinces' of Iraqi-Kurdistan, no matter the cost.[13]

Here is Ms Bell's personal appreciation in a letter to her father:

> The RAF has done wonders bombing insurgent villiages. It was even more remarkable than the display we saw last year . . . much more real . . . wonderful and horrible . . . [T]hey dropped bombs all round it, as if to catch the fugitives and finally fire bombs which even in the brightest sunlight made flares of bright flame in the desert. They burn through metal and water won't extinguish them. At the end the armoured cars went out to round up the fugitives with machine guns.[14]

After the 1917 October revolution Churchill wanted to bomb Russia and use the same weapons "against the rebellious tribes of northern India". "I am strongly in favour of using poisoned gas against uncivilized tribes," he declared in one secret memorandum (and) criticized his colleagues for their "squeamishness." This was in reference to "the top secret M Device", an exploding shell containing a highly toxic gas. "Among other reactions" the effects of the "M Device" were "uncontrollable vomiting, coughing up blood and instant, crippling fatigue."[15]

Forget the genocidal massacres and horrors perpetrated on the civilian population, deep down, in her heart of hearts, Gertrude Bell not only loved the people but the culture. The BBC also notes, in contemporary lingua, that Ms Bell "was into archaeology, map-making, photography [and] with her awe-inspiring skills . . . travelled across Arabia, mapping it as she went . . . inform[ing] the world's understanding of the Middle East and the various peoples who lived there."[16]

It is this extraordinary Brit-speak gobbledegook that people must heed in coming to terms with the reality of contemporary global politics, and how meaningful pressure may be brought to bear on the Turkish State. People thereabouts, and elsewhere in the world, have a different perception of the British way, and how they may learn from us on humanitarian issues in the contemporary world. After all, we still have a monarchy, an aristocracy and a House of Lords. The idea that an example may be set by the British system will produce little more than a horse-laugh, as it did to Mustafa Kemal Atatürk and his followers.

(2018)

# Notes

INTRODUCTION

1. https://www.institutkurde.org/en/info/the-kurdish-population-1232551004
2. The Kurdish Resistance in Exile by Mehmed Uzun, in *Autodafe, the Journal of the International Parliament of Writers*, Spring 2001.
3. For information on this visit http://www.freeocalan.org/news/english/interview-withlawyers-01-06-19
4. See the essay by Uzun, in *Autodafe 2*, p69.
5. Arming Repression: US Arms Sales to Turkey During the Clinton Administration, being a Joint Report of the World Policy Institute and the Federation of World Scientists, October 1999.
6. https://www.cnbc.com/2018/12/19/a-messy-multi-billion-dollar-weapon-sale-between-turkey-russia-and-the-us-just-got-more-complicated.html
7. Firsat Yildiz, 2001; see https://www.theguardian.com/uk/2001/aug/07/politics.immigration
8. Report on the State of Emergency Region, 1992, by the Human Rights Association branches and their representatives; this extract from the pamphlet *Gathering in Istanbul for Freedom of Expression: March 10–12, 1997* (published by the Freedom for Freedom of Expression Initiative, 1997).

9. In a press release by the Freedom of Thought Initiative. See the pamphlet *Gathering in Istanbul for Freedom of Expression: March 10–12, 1997*, op. cit.

10. *Em Hene!* is my translation into Kurmanji for the statement We Exist!

11. Also present on these 'benefit nights' were Alasdair Gray, Agnes Owens, Tom Leonard, Bernard MacLaverty; Sandie Craigie, Gordon Legge and Aonghas MacNeacail; Neville Lawrence, Suresh Grover, Kurdish musician Newroz and the Sativa Drummers. The events were supported strongly by Edinburgh's radical bookshop, Word Power Books.

12. In London and Wales among the participants were Moris Farhi, Vedat Türkali, Jack Mapanje (Malawe), and musician Dafydd Iwan. In autumn 2001 Dr Beşikçi was released from prison but punishments continued.

13. For a full account of this, see 'Byzantine Politics: The Abduction and Trial of Abdullah Öcalan' by William Clark, published as a Variant magazine supplement.

14. Ibid. citing the *New York Times*, 20 February 1999.

15. *The Kurdish Observer*, 28 November 1999.

16. See the campaign literature for Öcalan's fight for freedom, an 'international appeal' to writers and artists, February 1999.

17. For fuller information on the abduction and trial see the essays by Sheri Laizer, available through the internet.


## OPPRESSION AND SOLIDARITY

1. See p87, *A People Without a Country: the Kurds and Kurdistan*, edited by Chaliand, Gerard (Zed Press 1980).

2. The *Glasgow Keelie* was a radical newssheet created and distributed by the group known as Workers City that operated in the late 1980s and early 1990s.

## THE FREEDOM FOR FREEDOM OF EXPRESSION RALLY

1. Report from PEN International Writers in Prison Committee.
2. İsmail Beşikçi, *Selected Writings: Kurdistan & Turkish Colonialism* Kurdistan Solidarity Centre: Kurdistan Information Centre (London, 1991).
3. With France and Iran (Persia), the USA stayed somewhat in the background.
4. Ismet Sheriff Vanly's 'Kurdistan in Iraq', collected in *People Without a Country: the Kurds and Kurdistan* (London: Zed Press, 1980).
5. *Evening Times*, Glasgow newspaper, 21 April 1997, encouraging its readership to "fly to Turkey this autumn".
6. Amnesty International report.
7. From *Voice of Kurdistan* journal, whence this information is taken.
8. *The Kurds and Kurdistan: Thinking is a Crime*, a report on freedom of expression in Turkey, published by the International Association for Human Rights in Kurdistan (IMK), additional information from Voice of Kurdistan.
9. At Edinburgh University.
10. I had prepared for an audience I assumed would consist almost exclusively of Scottish people, but roughly 90% were Kurdish exiles.
11. My earlier 'Oppression and Solidarity', originally published in the collection *Some Recent Attacks* (AK Press, Edinburgh, 1992).

12. Except where stated, and with apologies to Kendal, the information here is lifted directly from a collection of essays published by Zed Press in 1979, reprinted a year later after the fall of the Shah of Iran, with an extra section: *People Without a Country: the Kurds and Kurdistan*, edited by Gerard Chaliand; Kendal's essay is entitled 'Kurdistan in Turkey'.

13. Among the literary works I presume proscribed in Turkey is my 1949 Penguin edition of Xenophon's *The Persian Expedition*. In his translation Rex Warner not only refers to 'Kurdistan', he refuses to censor or suppress Xenophon's account of his encounters in 400 BC with the 'Kardouçi' (which is spelled 'Carduchi').

14. See 'The Kurds in Syria' by Mustafa Nazdar in *A People Without a Country: the Kurds and Kurdistan*, Gerard Chaliand, Editor (Zed Press 1980).

15. For evidence of this read almost any issue of *Statewatch* journal (subscribe here http://www.statewatch.org/swonline.htm). A public meeting was held in 1997 in London on the issue of 'the Criminalisation of the Kurds in the UK and Europe'.

16. Information from *Statewatch* vol. 6, no. 6.

17. Later dropped the hyphenated part, now known as John Austin.

18. For a discussion of a South African/Turkish connection in the murder of Olof Palme, see *PSK Bulletin*, no. 6, November 1996.

19. *Statewatch*, vol. 7, no. 1.

20. Ibid., for an extended discussion on this.

21. *Lobster* magazine 32, for its comment on the *Mail on Sunday* report.

22. Linked directly to the British security services (MI6 in the early 1970s, MI5 after that). See *Lobster* 16, 19 for information on Paul Wilkinson and see also *Lobster* 10, 14 and others for a fuller account of the whole murky area. Wilkinson is an erstwhile colleague of far-right 'terrorist experts' such as Brian Crozier

and Maurice Tugwell. Subscribe to *Lobster* c/o Robin Ramsay (Dept W), 214 Westbourne Ave., Hull, HU5 3JB (email editor@ lobster-magazine.co.uk).

23. On 22 April 1997.
24. See *Kurdistan and Turkish Colonialism: Selected Writings*, İsmail Beşikçi (Kurdistan Solidarity Committee, 1991).
25. ibid.
26. Amnesty International report.
27. It may have been an oversight but I noted that none of the six Israeli writers was listed as having "knowingly and willingly consent[ed] to the publication of the *Mini Freedom of Expression* booklet".
28. Press releases by the Freedom of Thought initiative.
29. From the introduction to the *Mini Freedom of Expression* booklet.
30. Only as I understand it, as a layperson.
31. This involved students unfurling a banner in parliament.
32. A pseudonym adopted by the writer.
33. Famous Turkish musician and composer; former journalist; a leading human rights activist over the last three decades.
34. Amnesty International report, *Turkey: No Security Without Human Rights*.
35. *Kurdistan Information Bulletin* no. 34, January 1997. Just over four weeks after the event, on 16 April, Yurdatapan was detained at Istanbul Airport then held at the anti-terror branch of police headquarters.
36. ibid.
37. An introduction to his work, *Selected Writings: Kurdistan and Turkish Colonialism*, İsmail Beşikçi (Kurdistan Solidarity Committee, 1991).

### EM HENE!

1. It is worth noting that Italian politicians of the left were open in their support of the Kurdish people, and in the mid-1990s a major conference took place in Rome, attended by members of the Kurdish Parliament-in-Exile.
2. Amnesty International report.
3. ibid.
4. *Statewatch*, vol. 7, July–October 1997.
5. General Ahmet Çörekçi, quoted in an Amnesty International briefing entitled *Turkey: No Security Without Human Rights*.
6. *The Kurdistan Report* no. 27 for Hatip Dicle's report on this example of Turkish 'contra-guerrilla activity'.
7. If not for *Selected Writings: Kurdistan and Turkish Colonialism*, the little booklet put out by the KSC-KIC in 1991 in London, we would have nothing at all.
8. Crozier returned the compliment, describing Stone as "renowned Oxford historian".
9. *Lobster* no. 17 (1988), the essay 'Brian Crozier, the Pinay Circle and James Goldsmith', quotes at length from *Der Spiegel* no. 37 (1982) in an article called 'Victory for Strauss'. See also *Lobster* no. 18, 'The Pinay Circle and Destabilisation in Europe'.
10. ibid.
11. Former MI5 agent Cathy Massiter, on why she "had been required to resign from MI5", see Who Framed Colin Wallace?, Paul Foot (MacMillan, 1989).
12. See 'Covert Operations in British Politics 1974–78', *Lobster* no. 11. Note also John La Rose's reference to Kitson in my interview with him which can be found in my own *Selected Interviews* (thi wurd).

13. For the extended discussion of this, see Crozier's *A Theory of Conflict* (Hamish Hamilton, 1974), the chapter on 'The Problem of Subversion'.

14. Kemal in his 'Kurdistan in Turkey', see *People Without a Country: The Kurds and Kurdistan* (Zed Books, 1980); see also Crozier's *Free Agent: The Unseen War 1941–1991* (HarperCollins, 1993).

15. *Sunday Times*, 17 October 1971.

## WHAT IS IT THEY ARE TRYING TO EXPRESS?

1. A talk written for a PEN event that took place at the Scottish Poetry Library, 15 June 2016.

## WHO'S KIDDING WHO?

1. I regret very much that I came upon the Global Policy Forum too recently to impact on my work, including Peter Sluglett's *Britain in Iraq: 1914-1932* (London: Ithaca Press, 1976). See https://www.globalpolicy.org/iraq-conflict-the-historical-background. This also applies to H.C. Armstrong's *Grey Wolf: An Intimate Study of a Dictator*. Only this particular section features research from these sources.

2. See 'Sykes-Picot Agreement 1916'; 'The Proclamation of Baghdad March 11, 1917'; and '"The RAF Has Done Wonders" (1922, 1924)' at https://www.globalpolicy.org/iraq-conflict-the-historical-background-/36418.html

3. This is from *People Without A Country*, edited by Gerard Chaliand (Zed Books, 1980).

4. See p317 *Grey Wolf: Mustafa Kemal: An Intimate Study of a Dictator* by H. C. Armstrong.

5. ibid p317.

6. ibid p325.

7. ibid p326.

8. ibid p304.

9. ibid p311.

10. ibid p293.

11. See British Colonialism and Repression in Iraq, https://www. globalpolicy.org/iraq-conflict-the-historical-background-/36418. html

12. https://www.bbc.co.uk/programmes/profiles/373njzqGJGr5py-89ZQpMnxH/gertrude-bell

13. https://www.bbc.co.uk/programmes/profiles/373njzqGJGr5py-89ZQpMnxH/gertrude-bell

14. See https://www.globalpolicy.org/component/content/article/169/36378.html

15. https://www.theguardian.com/world/shortcuts/2013/sep/01/winston-churchill-shocking-use-chemical-weapons

16. https://www.bbc.co.uk/programmes/profiles/373njzqGJGr5py-89ZQpMnxH/gertrude-bell

# Selected Bibliography

Armstrong, H.C: *Grey Wolf: An Intimate Study of a Dictator* (Arthur Baker Ltd. 1932)

Beşikçi, İsmail: *Selected Writings: Kurdistan and Turkish Colonialism* (Kurdistan Solidarity Committee, 1991)

Chaliand, Gerard (edit.): *People Without a Country: the Kurds and Kurdistan* (Zed Press 1980)

Fernandes, Desmond: *The Kurdish and Armenian Genocides: from Censorship and Denial to Recognition?* (Apec Forlag 2007)

Hitti, Philip K.: *History of the Arabs; from the Earliest Times to the Present* (MacMillan & Co. 1963)

Hourani, A.H. and Stern, S.M. (edit.): *The Islamic City: A Colloquium* (Bruno Cassirer Ltd. 1970)

Miley, Thomas Jeffrey and Venturini, Frederico (edit.): *Your Freedom and Mine: Abdullah Öcalan and the Kurdish Question in Erdoğan's Turkey* (Black Rose Books 2018)

Öcalan, Abdullah: Three pamphlets published by International Initiative Editions 2013: *Democratic Confederalism, Liberating Life: Women's Revolution, War and Peace in Kurdistan*

Rizgar, Baran: *Learn Kurdish: A Multi Level Course in Kurmanji* (Lithosphere Print & Production Network 1996)

van Bruitnessen, Martin: *Agha, Shaikh and State: the Social and Political Structures of Kurdistan* (Zed Books Ltd. 1992)

# Further Reading and Study List, compiled by the Peace in Kurdistan committee: *Kobane, the Rojava Revolution and the Kurdish Struggle: Useful Resources*

Fascinated by the resistance in Kobane and want to know how it came about? Here you will find a whole set of resources to help guide you in your search for information on the historical struggle of the Kurdish people and the ideology that guides its practice.

## ON ABDULLAH ÖCALAN

Information on Abdullah Öcalan and some of his writings, including his pamphlets which are available in pdf format, can be found here: www.peaceinkurdistancampaign.com/resources/abdullah-Öcalan

Öcalan has written several books, only some of which have been translated into English:

- *Prison Writings Volume I: Roots of Civilization*, Abdullah Öcalan. January 2007.

- *Prison Writings Volume II: The PKK and the Kurdish Question in the 21st Century*, Abdullah Öcalan. March 2011.
- *Prison Writings Volume III: Roadmap to negotiations*, Abdullah Öcalan. January 2012.
- All publications can be found at: www.Öcalan-books.com

A review of all three *Prison Writings* by Felix Padel provides useful insights into the relevance of Öcalan's work: *The Kurdish Quest of Countering Capitalism to build a Democratic Civilisation*. Further writings by Öcalan and documents relating to his imprisonment can be found here: *www.freedom-for-Öcalan.com/english* A campaign for Öcalan's freedom from İmralı prison has been on-going for several years: *www.freeÖcalan.org*

## ON DEMOCRATIC AUTONOMY

BOOK: *Democratic Autonomy in North Kurdistan: The Council Movement, Gender Liberation, and Ecology* by TATORT Kurdistan and Janet Biehl (New Compass, 2013).

TAORT Kurdistan also wrote this article, 'Democratic Autonomy in Rojava', following a two-month visit to Rojava.

Janet Biehl, *Bookchin*, *'Öcalan and the Dialectics of Democracy'* (Paper given at the conference *Challenging Capitalist Modernity–Alternative Concepts and the Kurdish Quest*, which took place 3–5 February 2012 in Hamburg University.

Alexander Kolokotronis delves into the theoretical underpinnings of Democratic Autonomy, in *The No State Solution: Institutionalizing Libertarian Socialism in Kurdistan*.

This article by Rafael Taylor published in August 2014, 'The new PKK: unleashing a social revolution in Kurdistan', is a useful exploration of Öcalan's ideas and the theory and practice of democratic autonomy in Rojava.

Michael Knapp explains how the cooperative and democratic economic model being developed in Rojava offers possible emancipation from both capitalist and feudal systems of exploitation.

## ON THE KURDISH QUESTION IN TURKEY, THE PEACE PROCESS, AND THE CRIMINALISATION OF THE PKK

The Berghof Foundation recently published a report by Executive Member of the KNK, Adem Uzun, who was himself imprisoned on invented charges, called 'Living Freedom: The Evolution of the Kurdish Conflict in Turkey and the Efforts to Resolve It'.

A joint KNK and CENI – Kurdish Women's Office for Peace dossier, called 'Stop the political genocide and femicide against the Kurds in Turkey! Freedom for Abdullah Öcalan!', was published in February 2012 and gives a useful account of Turkey's AKP government's continued criminalisation of Kurdish activists; the violence of the state against women and the Kurdish women's movement's approach to combatting it; cross border military attacks; and the role and significance of Öcalan.

VIDEO: Havin Guneser, 'Constructive and Peaceful Solution to the Kurdish Question in Turkey of the Conference on the Kurdish Question in Turkey' (Paper given at the conference *The Kurdish Question in Turkey*, which took place at Queen University, Belfast on 17 April 2013.

Interview with Bese Hozat, Murat Karayılan and Cemal Bayık on the solution process, reproduced from ANF News, July 2013.

In an interview originally published in ANF in January 2013, KCK Executive Council President Murat Karaylian, speaks about the newest initiative for dialogue between the Kurdish movement and the Turkish government, which was announced in the days before the interview: Karayılan: Dialogue is important but there also needs to be a policy for resolution.

Marlies Casier and Joost Jongerden, 'Understanding today's Kurdish movement: Leftist heritage, martyrdom, democracy and gender', in European Journal of Turkish Studies.

Yvo Fitzherbert writes about the politics of the Kurdish language in Turkey.

VIDEO: Peace in Kurdistan Campaign's public event, *Turkey, Peace talks and the PKK: Freedom and Justice for the Kurds*, including speakers Ozlem Galip, Michael Gunter, Melanie Gingell and more.

One of the main demands of the Kurdish movement in the peace process is to remove the PKK from Turkish and international terrorism lists. The *Delist the PKK* campaign has been going on for over a year and our appeal continues to attract signatories. Here you can find articles related to the listing of the PKK.

The Campaign Against Criminalising Communities (CAMPACC), which campaigns to repeal the anti-terror law in the UK, has long advocated the delisting of the PKK. You can read their briefing on how their listing criminalizes the Kurdish community in the UK here: 'The UK ban on the PKK: Persecuting the Kurds'.

An interview with Zubeyir Aydar, 'The role of EU and US in Kurdish-Turkish conflict'.

This article by Vicki Sentas, 'Violence in Britain: how the war on terror criminalizes ordinary people', looks at the effects of PKK's continued listing on the Kurdish community in the UK.

In an ongoing 10-part series for the *Kurdish Question* called Surveillance, Targeting And The Criminalisation Of Kurds In The UK, author Desmond Fernandes analyses how security services and counterterrorism agencies have targeted the Kurdish community in London over the years. Part I: Introduction Part II: The New Penology of Risk Management.

### ON ROJAVA AND SYRIA

Kurdistan National Congress (KNK) Information File, published May 2014: 'Canton Based Democratic Autonomy of Rojava: A Transformation Process From Dictatorship to Democracy. The Democratic Autonomous Administration of Rojava' released a peace proposal for ending the conflict in Syria in May 2014, called 'Kurdish initiative for a democratic Syria'. The founding document of the Democratic Autonomous Administration of Rojava, *Charter of the Social Contract*, Rojava Cantons, 29 January 2014. Statement by the Kurdish Community Centre, Halkevi Turkish and Kurdish Community Centre, Sussex Kurdish Community Centre, Peace in Kurdistan Campaign & Campaign Against Criminalising Communities (CAMPACC), 14 February 2014.

### PEACE, EQUALITY AND SELF-DETERMINATION: THE KURDS TAKE THE LEAD IN PROPOSING A NEW WAY FOR SYRIA

Norman Paech, Emeritus Professor of Human Rights and former foreign policy spokesman for Die Linke, breaks down Turkey's hypocritical approach to Syria and it own Kurdish opposition movements in 'In the Glasshouse'.

David Morgan's articles for Live Encounters, 'The Mirage of ISIS' and 'The struggle against ISIS in historical perspective' are both excellent reviews of regional and global political dynamics following the rise of ISIS in Iraq and Syria.

Dilar Dirik, 'The 'other' Kurds fighting the Islamic State', published in Al Jazeera at the height of the Kobane resistance, asks why the 'other' Kurds of Syria (and their counterparts in Turkey) are still labeled as terrorists even while their superiority fighting ISIS has become widely acknowledged.

Yvo Fitzherbert excellent reporting from the region shows how Öcalan's ideas influenced the Rojava revolution and questions Turkey's disruptive policies towards the Kurds. His later article, published in February 2015, delves into how Turkey's unquestioning support for the Syrian opposition is effecting the Syrian refugees it is hosting.

VIDEO: BBC News documentary, *Syria's Secret Revolution*, released in November 2014, goes behind the front line fighting in Kobane to look at the social revolution taking place across Rojava.

Delegations have visited Rojava in recent months to offer solidarity to the struggle, find out more about what is happening and raise awareness of the revolution back in Europe. Janet Biehl took part in one such delegation organized by Civaka Azad and wrote this report on her return, 'Impressions of Rojava: A report of the Revolution', as well as providing further and more detailed eye-witness accounts of democratic autonomy in action. The whole group also published a collective statement in which they report that genuine democratic structures have been built in Rojava, which they believe can show a new way forward for Syria and the Middle East.

For anyone questioning whether the revolution is Rojava is genuine, David Graeber, anthropologist and political activist who took part in the delegation, answered the question clearly on his return.

Peace in Kurdistan Campaign has also organized delegations to the region, and published several of the delegate's reports once they returned.

Zaher Aarif travelled to North Kurdistan in November 2014 to find out more about the social revolution sweeping the region. He wrote about his visit for Anarkismo, where he describes how Kurdish institutions in the south of Turkey are operating autonomously in order to deal with the refugee crisis and continued attacks on the Kurdish people north and south of the border, just like in Rojava. Zaher notes that the social revolution taking place has come from local organisation of ordinary people on the ground.

Following the announcement on 26 January that Kobane had been liberated of ISIS troops, Trevor Rayne wrote that the Victory in Kobane was down to the will, determination, organisation and skill of the YPG and YPJ troops, and called for their affiliated organisation, the PKK, to be delisted.

### ON THE KURDISH WOMEN'S MOVEMENT

The KJB (Koma Jinên Bilind, translated as the High Women's Council) is an umbrella organisation of Kurdish women's organisations. Their website features an article, 'The Kurdistan Women's Liberation Movement for a Universal Women's Struggle', which explains the history and expansion of the Kurdish women's movement.

Abdullah Öcalan's booklet, *Liberating Life: Women's Revolution* is available as a pdf and is an essential read. Here he analyses the centrality of women's liberation from patriarchy in the struggle for a fully liberated society.

VIDEO: Dilar Dirik, 'Stateless Democracy: How the Kurdish Women Movement Liberated Democracy from the State' (Paper given at the New World Summit in Brussels, 21 October 2014).

'Kobane: the struggle of Kurdish women against Islamic State' is a useful article published in Open Democracy in October 2014 on the involvement of Kurdish women in the liberation of Rojava and the fight against ISIS.

Margaret Owen reports back following her visit to Rojava in December 2013. Her article, 'Gender, justice and an emerging nation: My impressions of Rojava', was published in Ceasefire Magazine soon afterwards.

Mary Davis, trade unionist and academic, spent 10 days visiting women's groups in northern Kurdistan (Turkey) in July 2012 as part of a delegation organized by CENI: http://peaceinkurdistan-campaign.com/activities/delegations/womens-solidarityjuly- 2012/

Dilar Dirik's 29 October article for Al Jazeera, 'Western fascination with 'badass' Kurdish women', goes beyond the western media's orientalising narrative of Kurdish women fighters in the YPJ to examine the history of women resistance fighters and their place in the PKK.

CENI – Kurdish Women's Office for Peace, based in Germany, released this 'Dossier on the Assassination of Three Female Kurdish Politicians in Paris' following the assassination of Sakine Cansiz, an icon of the Kurdish struggle for liberation, and two more of her activist colleagues. They were killed in broad daylight in the centre of Paris in early January 2013, just weeks after peace talks between the Turkish government and the PKK were announced.

Roj Women's Association, based in the UK, published this report in May 2012 which looks at state violence toward women human rights defenders in Turkey: 'A Woman's Struggle: Using Gender Lenses to Understand the Plight of Women Human Rights Defenders in Kurdish Regions of Turkey'.

## NEWS DIRECT FROM THE KURDISH PRESS

ANF News: https://anfenglish.com/news

Rojava Report: https://rojavareport.wordpress.com

Bianet: http://bianet.org/english

Dicle Haber: http://www.diclehaber.com/en

Support Kurds in Syria (UK based): http://supportkurds.org

Ronahi TV (in English): https://www.youtube.com/channel/UCnBX-zcAUpsLoaQq_xfyRmuQ

## A FURTHER LIST OF USEFUL BOOKS CAN BE FOUND AT PEACE IN KURDISTAN CAMPAIGN'S 'USEFUL READING' PAGE.

*The following websites are useful sources for further reading*

Peace in Kurdistan Campaign: www.peaceinkurdistancampaign.com

YPG International (an official information portal for the Rojava revolution and People's Defense Units, YPG): http://ypg-international.org/

Books by Abdullah Öcalan: http://www.ocalan-books.com

Free Öcalan: http://www.freeocalan.org

Scottish Solidarity with Kurdistan: http://www.sskonline.org.uk

Dusun Think: http://www.dusun-think.net

New Compass: http://new-compass.net

Truthout: https://truthout.org

Roarmag: https://roarmag.org

The Berghof Foundation: https://www.berghof-foundation.org

Kurdish Question: https://kurdishquestion.com

The Campaign Against Criminalising Communities: http://www.campacc.org.uk

Kurdish Institute: http://www.kurdishinstitute.be/english

The Conversation: https://theconversation.com/uk

Live Encounters: https://liveencounters.net

Yvo Fitzherbert: https://yvowrites.com

Z Communications: https://zcomm.org